Ocean
Without End

Ocean Without End

Book One
The Swashbuckler Trilogy

Kelly Gardiner

HarperCollins*Publishers*

For Tess, my princess,
and Conor, the finest swordsman of Anderson's Creek.

In memory of my grandfather, Bill Hegarty,
who took me to Station Pier on Saturday mornings
to see the ships, and sang to me of Galway Bay.

National Library of New Zealand Cataloguing-in-Publication Data

Gardiner, Kelly, 1961-
Ocean without end / Kelly Gardiner.
(Swashbuckler trilogy)
ISBN 1-86950-585-9
[1. Pirates—Fiction. 2. Slavery—Fiction. 3. Adventure and
adventurers—Fiction. 4. Napoleonic Wars, 1800-1815—Fiction.]
I. Title. II. Series: Gardiner, Kelly, 1961- Swashbuckler trilogy ; bk. 1.
NZ823.3—dc 22

First published 2006
Reprinted 2006
HarperCollins*Publishers* (NewZealand) Limited
P.O. Box 1, Auckland

ISBN 186950 585 9

Cover design by Stuart Horton-Stephens, Geeza
Cover illustration by Mark Wilson
Typesetting by Janine Brougham
Printed by Griffin Press, Australia, on 50 gsm Bulky News

Contents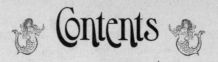

1.
The wraith ship

The attack began just after dawn.

It was dark when I woke up. I always loved this time of the day, before the noise began, before the fishmongers' cries went up and the cart wheels started grinding against the cobblestones. Lucas stirred and groaned in his bed by the fireplace, his pale red curls damp with sweat. I could hear our mother's deep, steady breathing across the other side of the room.

As the half-light crept in, shapes began to form, and our house came to life before my eyes, like some magical show put on especially for me. The mantelpiece emerged first from the darkness, its chipped limestone picking up the dawn and casting shadows onto the wall behind. The chairs became squarer and grew legs. On the table, last night's candle-wax had pooled itself into a pale crescent, and the buttons from Lucas's red jacket sat in a heap waiting to be sewn back on in the heat of the afternoon.

Mama rose silently and went outside with the water bucket and a spare flagon. She liked to beat the other women to the well in the *piazza*. 'Gossips,' she'd say, 'they're all such terrible gossips.' She hated how they talked about her behind her back. But then again, they talked about everyone. It was just their way of passing the time.

'No point pretending, Mama,' I'd said one day. 'Father's gone, and everyone knows it.' I knew from her expression that I shouldn't talk of it again. I never did, until — but I'm jumping ahead of my story. We must go back to the beginning, to that morning.

Sleepyhead Lucas finally stirred himself, laughing as he climbed up onto my bunk.

'You should see your hair, Lil,' he said. 'It's sticking straight up.'

'At least it's clean — not like yours, you smelly thing.'

'Let's go for a swim before breakfast,' he said. 'Sun's out. It's getting hot already.'

I pushed open the shutter, and we leaned out our window, gazing across the old harbour studded with the usual fishing boats and coastal traders.

There, riding high on the current, was the most glorious ship we'd ever seen.

She was tall, the quarterdeck fifty feet above the waterline and her masts higher than any tree. Gold and red paintwork gleamed against the dull grey water. Her figurehead was a woman with golden hair, floating in the early morning mist.

Lucas and I ran down to the quay to watch her boats unload. Such a ship, we cried as we ran, must be laden with rubies and spices. Such a ship must have flown here from heaven, or even from Holland. Such a ship must be filled with fine brave men in bright blue uniforms with buttons as shiny as their cannon.

It wasn't.

We watched as the harbour-master's barge picked its way through the fishing boats to greet the mighty newcomer.

'Come on,' shouted Lucas. 'Let's row out there too!'

But something wasn't right.

There was no line of uniformed men on deck to greet the harbour master, no bosun to pipe him aboard with a squealing silver whistle. No flag. No bustle aboard.

I grabbed Lucas's hand and held him back as he tried to scramble down the worn stone causeway to our boat, *Swallow*.

'Let me go!' he cried. 'What's wrong with you?'

'Wait a minute,' I cautioned. 'We can't go out there.'

'I can. You're not the boss of me.'

I held him tighter, and he wriggled like an eel. 'Let go. Just because you're older doesn't mean —'

'Shut up, Lucas, and wait a moment. Have you ever seen such a ship?'

'Of course not. That's why I want to row over and see it.'

'Be quiet and look carefully. They've cleared the decks for action. But it's not a warship, at least not from the British Navy.'

He sighed and stood still at last. I watched the ship. The gun ports were open, and the cannon muzzles had been run out ready to fire. But there was still no sign of anyone on board, as if it were a ghost ship that had floated in during the night, deserted and still.

'Weird,' muttered Lucas.

Weird and silent. Until the fat little harbour master in his brass buttons and red hat drew alongside and shouted up, angry at being ignored.

There was a puff of smoke from the scuppers, and a single shot that echoed around the port long after the harbour master fell face first into the water and floated there. His boat crew sat still in terror. The harbour held its breath.

Then hell broke loose upon us all.

Cannon in the ship's starboard bow exploded in a burst of flame and smoke and noise, while others took aim at the guardhouse on the quay and blew the red tiles off the roof. All the ship's big guns were firing now, as fast as they could reload, and men swarmed up the ropes into the tops to take aim with muskets. The air was filled with shot.

In the streets along the waterfront, people ran everywhere, like ants in a rainstorm. The postmaster's horse reared up and raced through the streets, its carriage careering crazily behind. The walls of the old fort, made of stone many feet thick, burst at each cannonade and crumbled like dry bread. Market stalls flew through the air, scattering baskets, lemons and plums onto the cobblestones.

I pulled Lucas down behind the huge bronze lion that guards the Customs House. We watched between its jaws as the town burst into flames around us. Lucas was quiet now, panting as if he'd run up the mountain. We saw one and then another of the garrison guards race out of the gatehouse and crumple to the ground.

'Why are they shooting at us?' Lucas shouted

over the crashing guns. 'Who are they?'

'I don't know.' I was trembling a little. 'We'd best run home, quickly. Mama will be beside herself.'

We sprinted up the steps and ducked behind the low wall that ran along the top of the quay. Lucas peeped over one last time.

'There are dead people everywhere!'

There was a clamour of footsteps behind us, and we squeezed ourselves against the wall to let the guards rush by. Some of them were still buckling on their swords, and more than one seemed very scared.

'There goes Flynn,' Lucas shouted. 'Hey, Flynn!'

One of the younger soldiers waved and shouted at us. 'You two get home. What on earth are you doing here?'

I nodded and took Lucas's hand. It was sweaty, and he gripped tight.

'We're going,' I told Flynn. 'Don't you do anything brave yourself.'

Flynn smiled nervously. 'Not likely.' I'd never seen him like this. He'd grown up, almost overnight, since he'd joined the army.

'Who are they, Flynn? Frenchies?' asked Lucas.

'Mark the flag. You'll see.'

We turned back towards the ship. A huge black pennant now flew from the topmast; sewn onto it was a grinning yellow skeleton brandishing a cutlass.

'Pirates!' cried Lucas. 'But why would they attack Santa Lucia?'

I shook my head. Nothing made much sense today.

'Maybe it's old Blackbeard, come to kidnap you.'

Flynn slapped me on the shoulder and winked (rather bravely, I thought).

'Don't worry, Lucas. One old ship can't take on a whole town garrison. It'll be over in an hour, you'll see.' He straightened his sword-belt, waved, and ran to catch up with his squadron.

We waited until the guards had clattered down the stairs and made our way back up through the twisting lanes. Behind us, the incredible roar of the ship's cannon was answered by the guns from the fort on the hill.

Our mother was standing in the lane outside our cottage, waiting. As soon as we turned the corner, she started running towards us, calling out. 'There you are! I feared you were dead.' She grabbed us both in her arms and held us tightly to her.

'We're safe, Mama.'

'My sweets, can't you hear the noise? The port is under attack.'

'We know,' Lucas piped up. 'We saw everything. There were dead people. And pirates.'

'Saints in heaven . . . ' she began, but her temper got the better of her. 'Damn them!'

'It's all right, Mama, really. The guards are out on the ramparts, and the fort is firing all its guns.' I tried to reassure her, but she still gripped my arm and stared out towards the water.

'We must flee. Come, pack your things.'

'But Mama, Flynn said —'

'Pay no mind to Flynn. He's young — you're all too young to remember the last such time.' She started pulling us, running, towards our house. 'We'll go up into the hills. I know a cave where we can hide.'

'Cave? What cave?'

'Never mind. Quickly now. Lucas, see if you can coax the chickens into a basket. Lily, you help me gather some food. Roll some warm clothes up in your blankets. And hurry!'

There was no arguing. Lucas ran out into the back yard to deal with the chickens, stubborn brutes that they were. Mama and I grabbed a cheese, grapes, onions, salted fish, some bread, our bowls and knives, and wrapped it all up in one of her shawls. Outside, in the lane, people rushed back and forth seeking news and reassurance. We were the only ones who seemed to be packing.

Mrs Brisket from next door passed our window and peered in. 'Frances,' she said, 'where are you going?'

Mama stopped only for a moment. 'I'm taking the children up into the hills.'

'Don't be silly, dearie. You'll freeze. The wolves will get you.'

'I'd rather wolves and wild cats than being burned in my bed, or worse.'

Mama brushed a strand of hair from her forehead. She looked so fine, standing there, her black eyes defiant. I'd never seen her like this.

'Now, now, Frances, please,' Mrs Brisket pleaded. 'If you're worried about the little ones, come and stay with us. You're safer behind the town walls than in the mountains.'

'Thank you, but really, I must,' said Mama. 'We must. I've lost a husband to pirates, Mrs Brisket. I will not lose my children as well.'

I must have gasped aloud. Both women turned to me, and Mama moved close to put her arm around my shoulders. 'Lily, I'm sorry, but it's time you knew the truth,' she said. 'Now come along, or we'll all be pirate slaves.'

'You told us he died,' I said, accusingly.

'So he did, in a way.' Her voice was quiet and steady. 'We'll talk more of this later, my love. Come now. Grab your cloak and let's be off.'

'He was a fine man, your father,' Mrs Brisket called from the window. 'Don't ever let anyone tell you otherwise. If you need shelter, any of you, our home is yours. Remember that.'

Mama smiled. 'Thank you, Nancy. You're very kind.'

Lucas appeared with some very grumpy hens in a basket too big for him to carry. He dragged it up the steps and into the centre of the room.

'Attila pecked me, so I left him behind.'

'Let's leave him for the pirates, then, shall we?' said Mama. 'All that squawking and bluster. They deserve each other.'

'Aye,' Lucas said, laughing. 'That rooster's a black-hearted devil. He'd be a match for any pirate king.'

Mama hoisted the hen basket onto her back. 'You'll have to manage the food parcel, Lily. Can you do that?'

I nodded, still stunned by what she'd said, but picked up the bundled shawl.

'Lucas, take the cider flagon,' said Mama. 'You can lead the way. Off we go.'

She was trying to make it seem like an adventure,

and it was in a way, so Lucas skipped ahead happily, telling Mama every detail of what we'd seen that morning. She listened carefully.

But as we made our way up through the back streets and out into the fields behind the town, I felt burdened by more than just the load on my back.

My father, taken by pirates? They must have murdered him. But why? He was a fisherman, did no harm to anyone. Perhaps that was it. He was poor, and it wasn't worth trying to get ransom money from a family with no gold or rich relations — no relations at all, as far as I knew.

I could hardly remember his face now. But I remembered his hands, so rough from the ropes and the fishing lines. I remembered his terrible smelly green cap that Mama tried to throw out in the hope he wouldn't notice. I remembered him flinging me up into the air — make me fly, Papa, make me fly!

I remembered those awful months after he vanished. Mama would watch the quay every afternoon, waiting for his boat to pull in. I was so small then, and Lucas was hardly even walking. We'd all curl up at night in the same bed, and in the dark hours Mama would sob and I'd wrap myself around her, clinging like a barnacle, trying to make it better.

It was so many years ago now — maybe six or more. I don't remember when I gave up on him, but Mama didn't give up for years. While Lucas and I grew and clamoured and forgot his face, our splendid, spirited mother slowly shrank into a worn-out washerwoman who stood in line at the water pump and ignored the chattering of the women around her. But she still read to us every evening, her face alight with adventures, and drew with chalk on our flagstone floors. She taught us our lessons at the kitchen table, something different every day — how to write music, or which mushrooms were good to eat, or gruesome stories about the emperors of Rome.

Sometimes she told us about all the places she'd seen when she was young, sailing with her father all over the ocean — about the whales and the flying fish, about golden cities and great palaces, about volcanos and mountains covered in snow, about battles and huge storms and battered ships. She still sang Lucas to sleep every night, their faces close together, until his eyelids finally drooped and his smile softened into dreaming.

But she was weary to her bones, and every Sunday morning, when everyone else was at Mass and the bells were ringing in the towers, she walked alone to the headland and stared out to sea. Lucas and I followed her once and hid behind a tree to spy on her. But he got bored, and I got a creeping guilty feeling as if I'd sneaked into the cathedral all by myself. We weren't supposed to be there. It was Mama's private time. We crept away and never said a word, but I swore to myself I would never let anyone hurt my mother ever again.

She was sad enough already. Papa had gone down in a storm, somewhere off Malta, they told me. There was no sign of him now, no sign even of the old blue boat. The *Cygnet*, he'd called it, a joke about our name. Rafe Swann and his little ship, the *Cygnet*.

'One day,' he'd said, 'I'll have a great ship. That'll

be a ship worthy of a Swann. In the meantime, I'll make do with the *Cygnet*, the mightiest but smallest ship in Santa Lucia.'

He'd smiled, blue eyes gazing at the horizon as always. I do remember that.

2.
Flight to the Lion Cave

We tramped for an hour up a dusty track into the hills, then Mama led us off through some bushes, skirting huge limestone boulders, and into a valley. A narrow goatherd's path threaded along the side of the hill and down towards the stream. Even here we could hear the cannon, still firing in the distance.

Lucas was tiring quickly, so we sat down under an old cedar to munch on some bread. Nobody spoke much. We were all too exhausted.

Mama roused us, and we pressed on again, dipping down into the valley and then heading up a steep climb to the very top of a boulder outcrop everyone called Lion Rock. You could see it from all over the island, but I'd never been so close to it before. As we clambered up the last few steps underneath the lion's mane, Lucas gave a yell and ran forward. 'It really is a cave. Woo-hoo!'

Mama followed him into the darkness, calling out. 'Watch out for snakes. They probably haven't had any company up here for years.'

'There's an old fireplace. See, Lil?' Lucas shouted. 'Someone's been here. There's fish bones everywhere.'

I turned around and looked back along the way we'd come. The path was invisible from here. A few miles away, the old stone town nestled around the harbour. The water still glistened in the sun, and out to sea the fishing boats bobbed on the gentle ocean.

All my life, there had been alarms of wars and pirates approaching our island, Santa Lucia, and on many a moonlit night there were smugglers in the rocky coves around the coast. Many's the time the fishing fleet had kept to its harbour for fear of being taken by Arab marauders. But the town itself, with its fine ramparts and English garrison, had never been attacked. Not in my memory, anyway.

It was a different place now, filled with gunfire and explosions. From up here, it looked as if the quayside warehouses were on fire, with great clouds of black smoke billowing up. The cannon on the hill were pouring shot down into the harbour, where boats were aflame and the great ship still floated, further out of range now, firing its massive guns.

Our little island was no longer a safe haven in these dangerous waters.

I waited until it was dark and Lucas was asleep before moving closer to Mama to ask the question that had troubled me all afternoon.

'What really happened to Papa?'

She stared at the tiny campfire we'd built in the shelter of the cave.

I waited for her to speak, but it was a long time before she began.

'I don't know. That was the worst of it, never really knowing what happened.'

'What did they tell you?' I urged. 'You must have heard something.'

'It's all very confused.' She stoked the fire with a burnt stick. 'I heard so many tales. First, I heard he was taken as a slave by corsairs, probably from Tripoli. But there was one story that he'd given too much trouble and been marooned on a rocky island somewhere in the middle of the ocean. Someone told me they'd found a body . . . a skeleton. Once I heard he was still alive and sailing along the Barbary Coast. But I just can't be sure if it was really him.'

'So he might still be alive somewhere?' My eyes searched her face for clues.

'If he was alive, he'd have come home by now. Only slavery or death would keep him away from us. I want you to remember that.' She was grinding the stick deep into the ashes of the fire, sending sparks floating up to the blackened roof of the cave.

'They weren't corsairs,' I said.

'What do you mean?' She was watching me closely.

'The ship that attacked us this morning. It wasn't a Barbary galley — it looked more like a Spanish or Dutch ship. So you don't have to worry that the corsairs have come back to take us.'

She smiled, just a little.

'Pirates are pirates, my darling girl, whether they are raiders from Algiers taking Christian slaves, or Knights of Malta capturing Muslim slaves, or just fishermen down on their luck. It's best to be safe out of their way.'

'I don't understand why they've attacked the town. It makes no sense.'

'Perhaps there's gold in the fort, or maybe it's just gunpowder they're after.'

'They've used enough of that today.'

'Aye, indeed,' she said. 'Maybe they were just hungry, and the sight of a market town made their mouths water. Some pirates don't need a reason.'

'What would my father have done, if he'd seen them attack this morning?' I wondered aloud.

'He'd have sent us up here, and then gone down to fight anyone he could lay his hands on.'

Mama laughed at some memory she couldn't share.

'We used to come up here many a time, before you were born. Life was much more dangerous then. We lived through many days such as this when I was your age, when the seas were filled with marauders and not a month went by without a ship taken, people killed — your grandparents amongst them. But the last few years, with all those French and British Navy ships sailing about battling each other, the pirates seemed to vanish. I suppose they'd gone off to harass some other poor folk. Now they've come back. Mrs Brisket, bless her, and the others, they've forgotten how it used to be. But not me. I'll never forget.'

I was feeling sleepy now and nestled down beside her, my head in her lap. She stroked my hair.

'My father wouldn't be afraid of pirates,' I murmured.

'No, he was never afraid. It got him into strife, but I loved him for it.'

'I don't remember him very well,' I confessed.

'Never fear, my darling girl,' she whispered. 'I'll remember for both of us. Now, sleep.'

I woke in the dark a few hours later. The dusty cave floor was hard as marble, and damp as winter. Every muscle hurt.

Down below in Santa Lucia township, the shooting had finally stopped, although from time to time, as I lay with my arms wrapped tight around me, I could hear a musket firing from the ramparts.

There was a glimmering of moonlight outside the cave. I struggled to my feet and tiptoed out. The town was quiet, but not still. It was an ancient groaning beast, stirring to defend itself from attack. Beyond it, the ocean shimmered silver, and against the light was a familiar shape — the pirate ship, tacking around Seal Rock outside the harbour. They were leaving.

I skipped down the hill to watch them go, and settled on a tussock where I could see the whole bay and clear out to sea. My whole body relaxed with a breath, so completely that I realised that I'd been tight with fear all day. Somewhere a nightingale sang. What a perfect night. There was just enough of a breeze to see the pirates on their way, and enough light for me to watch them go.

I thought of my friend Flynn, his hands tight around a musket, peering into the dark across the harbour. But perhaps he was wounded. Or dead.

Like my father. Or was my father marooned on a lonely rock somewhere in the vast Mediterranean? Somewhere near Malta. Waiting for someone to come to his rescue. Waiting for Lucas and me to come to his rescue.

As soon as we're old enough we'll go in search of him, I whispered into the darkness. As soon as we can buy some provisions and a bigger boat, we'll set sail to find our father. If he's still alive.

I wasn't watching the path. I wasn't even listening to the sounds around me. Still, I don't know how they crept up so close without me hearing. First thing I heard was the click of the musket being cocked just behind me.

'Now then, what are you doing out here all alone?' someone whispered.

I turned around very slowly, hardly daring to breathe.

In the darkness I could make out a few faces, all strangers, all filthy and ragged. One of them aimed a blunderbuss right at me. 'Answer me, boy!' he hissed.

I swallowed and tried to speak, but no noise came.

The men took a step closer. One, bald and toothless, was glaring at me. The others peered around carefully, as if fearing an ambush.

'Ah, take him down to the boat.'

'He'll slow us down. Just shoot 'im.'

'No noise. Cut his throat, and quick about it.'

I jumped to my feet. 'No!' I tried to scream, but it came out as a whisper.

One man, taller than the others, stepped forward, right up to me, close enough for me to smell him. He smelled rotten.

He brandished a dagger in my face.

'Right then, son. You can show us the path to Cockle Bay, or we'll kill you on the spot.'

I nodded. This was no time to tell them I'm not a boy.

'I know the way,' I whispered. 'You're not on the right path. It's down there a-ways.'

'Lead on, then, and quick about it.'

I nodded again and motioned for them to follow — to follow me away from Mama and Lucas, safe and asleep in their cave. I stumbled through the gorse, cutting around the bottom of the hill and towards the cliff that sheltered Cockle Bay.

I could hear the strangers shuffling behind me, but they were very quiet. Two of them hauled something heavy along between them. No smugglers, these. It must be a raiding party from the ship.

They must be pirates.

'Boy!' called the tall man. 'Stop a minute.'

I waited for him to catch up.

He didn't have such an evil face, close up, but there was a pistol stashed in his belt and his dagger was still drawn and at the ready.

'I've lost my bearings, lad. You'd better not be leading us astray. Where's the bay?'

'Down there,' I pointed. 'You just follow this path around the cliff and watch out for the track down over the rocks.'

'Tell me, did you ever hear of a lion cave around here somewheres?'

'We don't have lions here, sir, not for years,' I said. 'But there are caves everywhere. Hundreds of them.'

'This one's up on a hill. It's a special sort of cave.'

'Sorry, sir, no idea,' I shook my head. 'Must be a secret cave.'

'All right then. It doesn't matter. We're late enough already. Lead on.'

'You can see the path from here,' I said, hopefully.

'You go first. No tricks and no running off. Nobody will hear if I shoot you now.'

I plodded ahead, trying desperately to imagine Cockle Bay and recall if there were any hiding holes in the cliffs. If I ducked behind the rocks and then dived into the water, they wouldn't bother to chase me. Not in the dark. Not if they were already late. Late for what, though?

We reached the track and started down the cliff, slipping and sliding on the pebbles. I heard cursing behind me as someone tripped. Nobody was bothering to keep their voices down now.

Below us, on the beach, a knot of men waited by a small boat. One of them waved up, and the tall man whistled in recognition.

My feet touched the sand. I had to run now, or never, before the two crews met up. I looked about me for a place to hide — there, to the left, a boulder with the waves coursing around it. I braced for the sprint.

Something whacked me on the back of my head. Hard. There was a cracking noise in my skull, and I started to run, but my legs turned to water beneath me and suddenly I was on my face in the sand and somebody was dragging me feet first across the beach. I heard myself groan, with sickening pain circling my head and rocks and shells gouging into my skin.

Next thing I remembered was the bottom of the boat, my face in a pool of water and what tasted like blood. Maybe it was my blood — it was too dark to tell. When I tried to feel the back of my head, my arms wouldn't work. They were numb.

No, they were tied behind my back.

There was laughter in the boat, relief by the sound of it. Whatever these pigs had planned, it sounded like they'd carried it off, along with me and whatever was in the bundle. Deep in my stomach was something like despair. Something worse.

I groaned, thinking of Mama waking up to find me gone, spirited away — another Swann taken by bloody pirates.

'Hey, Jem, it sounds like your new cabin boy's awake,' someone said.

'That's a bleedin' miracle, seeing as how hard you clobbered him.'

Somebody sniggered. 'He's lucky he's not one of them port guards. We don't hit them, do we? We slits their pretty clean throats.'

They laughed. That's the kind of thing pirates find very funny — don't ask me why.

'There she is, coming around the headland,' called the tall man.

'Aye, Jem.'

'Avast oars. We'll wait for her to come to us.'

I glanced up. They were all staring eastwards. There, dark against the moon, was the ship.

One last chance. One deep breath.

And over the side. Somehow I managed it — I don't know how. I pushed myself up and over. One foot caught on the gunwale, and I heard curses as the boat rocked violently. Then I was in the water.

It was freezing, but that brought me to my senses. My legs thrashed to keep me afloat as I struggled away from the boat, like a beetle in a pond. Two of the men had been flung in the water by the sudden movement, and were floundering around trying to get back on board. They were all shouting, oars banging every which way, and the old fellow let off a musket into the air. In the stern, the tall man, the one they called Jem, stood and watched me swim away.

I turned my back on them to concentrate on kicking my legs. God, it was hard. With each push my head went under. My arms were useless, tied tight and no way of getting them free. I was swimming nowhere, just swallowing water, spluttering, sinking and weeping now in desperation.

'Please, please,' I cried.

Strong hands grabbed at my jacket and hoisted me back aboard the boat, just as the shadow of the great ship fell across us.

3.
The cabin boy

'What the hell are you shooting at?' a voice called down from the deck.

'Nothing, sir,' Jem shouted. 'Just old Brasher getting carried away in all the excitement.'

'Get them aboard, and let's get out of this hole,' came the order.

Ropes were flung down and fastened bow and stern. As the crew hauled us up in the creaking, jolting boat, the ship came about. She was setting out to sea.

Jem put his face close to mine.

'Listen to me,' he whispered. 'Keep your head down, don't answer back and don't be jumping into the water every time my back is turned. I'm telling you this for your own good.'

I just stared at him.

I was a captive. A pirate slave.

He shook me.

'Did you hear me?'

I nodded.

'What's your name, boy?'

My name?

'Lucas,' I said. 'Lucas Swann.'

'Right, then, Lucas Swann. You're plucky enough, but maybe not as smart as you think, so do what you're told and everything will work out.'

I gazed back towards the dark shape of the island. My home, my mother, even my name — everything had been taken from me in one moonlit moment.

'I'm Jem McGuire, first mate.'

I said nothing. We were nearly level with the rails. I could hear the clamour on board, the heaving and shouting.

'You're no relation of Rafe Swann, are you?' Jem whispered.

'He was my father.'

Jem scowled. 'Tell no one. Make up a new name. That's no name to be using on the *Gisella*.'

Gisella. Such a pretty name for such a dastardly ship.

The boat banged to a halt, and the crew clambered out. Jem pushed me so I fell over the gunwales and onto the deck of *Gisella*.

'That's the way he likes to get out of boats,' he joked. 'Head first.'

'A captive, eh, Jem?' said someone who looked fearsome even in the dark, with bright red hair, long and plaited, and a moustache as wide as a hearth broom. 'Don't seem like he'd be worth much.'

'Cabin boy, I figured, since young Tommy got himself killed.'

'Oh, aye, fair enough.'

Dozens of figures ran about the deck in the dark, or shuffled in long lines to haul on heavy ropes. Others lifted the boat and lashed it tightly against the massive mast. Suddenly the murmur of voices fell, and Jem straightened up to face the quarterdeck.

'Did you get them?' It was the same rough voice that had hailed us before.

'Aye, sir. We got 'em, no trouble. There was only a few guards left around the back of town, just as you planned.'

'Good.'

'Only we couldn't find the cave, sir, so we couldn't hide them — we've brought it all on board.'

There was a moment of silence. The voice grew nearer.

'Blasted fools. Can't do a damned thing right, any of you. Well, have them locked in my cabin.'

Jem nodded. 'I will, Captain.'

A huge man with a vast beard and bushy black eyebrows glared down from the quarterdeck. 'What's that you have there?'

'New cabin boy, sir.'

The captain stared intently at me. Even in the moonlight, I could see his glassy eyes gleam.

'Ha!' He laughed. 'Cabin girl, don't you mean?'

'Hey?' said Jem. He grabbed my arm and spun me around to face him.

'Jesus! It is a girl.'

There was more laughter from the deck.

'Well, well, Jem, trying to sneak her on board, eh?' teased the old fellow from the landing party.

'No such thing,' said Jem, flustered. 'He told me his name was Lucas. I mean, she did. Anyway, it's dark — how was I to know?'

'Either way, it's no use to us,' said the captain. 'Look

at it — too poor for a ransom, too damn skinny to sell for a slave, and too young for anything else. Throw it overboard. We're far enough out to sea now for her to be telling no tales.'

A couple of the men from the boat crew muttered to each other.

'I'll do it,' said one. 'She's been a right pain already. Tipped me overboard.'

'Aye,' murmured the old fellow, 'she's feisty enough. Led us down to the beach all right though, I'll give 'er that. We was lost coming over that hill.'

My hands were clenched now around a rope behind me, my arms still tied fast. I would not give up without a fight. The big man with red hair strode towards me.

'Give her to me, I'll do the job proper. You lot go get dry.'

'Listen, Miller,' Jem said to the redhead, 'she could still be a cabin boy till we get ourselves a real one.'

'You heard the captain.'

They both stared at me.

'No such thing as a cabin girl, anyhow. It wouldn't be proper,' said Miller.

I gulped some air and spoke out. 'I can sail. And fish.'

Miller laughed. 'We can all do that, lass. That's what we do when we're not burning and pillaging. We don't need any little girls to show us how to sail.'

'Then I can cook. And sew a little. Although I don't like to, much. But I bet you can't all cook.'

They simply stood and looked at me. I stared back, trying to remember every detail in case I needed to find them later amongst all these strange men. Jem was pale, with long stringy hair pulled back in a knot, and a stubbly beard. His loose white blouse was filthy, I could see that even in the dark, and it hung in tatters over green breeches. Miller was just as shabby, a bear of a man in a dark shirt open almost to his waistband, but in spite of his gruffness his laughter had been warm and lively.

Suddenly Miller bellowed, 'Carlo!'

A boy appeared at his elbow.

'Take her down to the galley and see if Cook can use a hand,' Miller growled. 'But mind, if he don't want her, bring her right back up here and she'll feed the sharks instead of us.'

There was a tugging at my arms as Jem loosened the ropes around my wrists.

'You behave yourself, now,' he whispered. 'Remember what I said.'

I nodded, and the boy grabbed my sleeve and dragged me towards the ladder. Everything was happening at great speed — one minute I was a boy, then a girl, then shark bait, and now a cook. I had no idea what would happen next, but at least I had a reprieve for a while, until I could figure out how to escape.

It was filthy inside the bowels of the ship, and the stench was enough to make me gag. The boy Carlo chattered nervously as we ran through the crew's quarters and clambered over drying sails.

'Watch your step here. I don't know what Cook will say. Goodness. I don't know what the captain will say when he finds you still here.'

'What's his name?' I asked.

'Why, El Capitán de Diablo, of course, the most bloodthirsty pirate in the Mediterranean.'

'Never heard of him.'

Carlo was aghast. 'Don't be ridiculous. Everyone's heard of him. He's famous.'

'Not in these parts.'

'Not so loud,' he warned. 'I don't think he'd like to hear you say that.'

'But it's true.'

'Pirates don't care for the truth. We're lying scoundrels.'

'Are you quite mad?' I asked. 'You sound as if you were proud of it.'

'A pirate's life is the best life there is,' said Carlo, puffing out his chest like a blowfish.

'Really? So you're an experienced pirate, are you?' He was just a few years older than me, soft black curls hanging down over his eyes. He looked nothing like a pirate — more like one of those silly young nobles who hang about the *piazza* and pretend to have swordfights. He even wore shoes, probably the only pair on board.

'Oh yes, I've been in two battles now.'

'Have you ever seen what happens to people when a cannonball hits them?'

He didn't even blink. 'Um, not really, no.'

'I have, just this morning. It was horrible.' I held onto his arm to stop him from running ahead of me. 'How long have you been a pirate, anyway?'

'About three weeks.'

I couldn't help smiling.

'How come you're here with all these maniacs?' I asked. 'Did you just march on board and sign up as crew?'

'Not exactly.'

'Well?'

'Actually, I'm a prisoner, same as you. They lock me up in the cabin when there's proper fighting. But I've been here longer, so you have to do what I say. They're ransoming me, I think. My father will have to pay ten thousand *scudi* to have me released.'

'Ten thousand! My God, who are you? Some kind of prince?'

'It's quite a lot, isn't it?' Carlo said proudly. 'Although I don't think my father has anything like that much money, so I have no idea what will happen. I expect they'll let me stay on as a crew member. I was a bit seasick at first, but it's a fine life once you get used to just floating around shooting at things. Now, here's the galley, so allow me to introduce you to —'

The door to the galley was completely filled by the fattest person I had ever seen in my life. Cook's enormous face was red and streaming with sweat, his thin hair plastered against his skull.

'What do we have here?' he asked.

I smiled at him. I never felt less like smiling, what with the ache in my head, and the bruises on my wrists, and being dragged away from my home and, well, everything. But I smiled as sweetly as I could.

'I'm Lily,' I said. 'Jem and Miller thought perhaps I could give you a hand with the cooking.'

'You don't look like no lily to me,' bellowed Cook.

'I am. Honest. I'm Lily Swann.'

Damn. It just came out.

'You don't look like no swan neither. Maybe one of them funny baby swans, just born like, all bedraggled and fluffy. What do they call 'em?'

'Cygnets,' said Carlo, helpfully.

'Eh?'

'That's a baby swan — a cygnet.'

'Bless my soul,' said Cook. 'There's a thing I never heard. Why aren't they called swanlings? Or swanlets? That's what comes of having a young lord aboard ship, you see. Something new to learn all the time.'

Carlo was beaming.

Cook waved me into the light. 'Let's have a look-see at you, then, all dripping wet and covered in blood as you are. That's your blood, I suppose?'

'I got hit on the head.'

'Who hit you?' said Carlo.

'Not sure. Jem, I think.'

'Never mind that now,' said Cook. 'We'll get it cleaned up soon enough. How old are you?'

'Twelve or thereabouts.'

'A little swan, eh? You're no relation to Rafe Swann, are you?'

Funny how you never hear a word of a person for years and then all at once people won't shut up about him.

'Rafe?' I pulled a face as if I was thinking hard. 'No, never heard of him. Never heard of any Swann but me.'

'Just as well for you, girly,' said Cook. 'Captain

didn't get on with Rafe Swann. Not at all. So don't go mentioning that name. I wouldn't anyway, if I was you.'

'I won't,' I assured him. Not until I figured out what on earth was going on and why everyone kept asking about my father.

'Well, then, Miss Cygnet, I suppose you won't eat much, so you may as well stay on. You can sleep there under the bench. Now, you say goodnight to your beau, and get out of my way while I gets the captain's oats on. They'll all be hungry as horses and yelling for their gruel any moment now.'

Carlo flushed bright red and ran off down the passage. Cook somehow squeezed himself back into the steaming galley and motioned for me to follow.

'First rule of ship cooking — never let the fire go out unless there's a fight on,' he warned. 'Second rule — never be late with the food when the watch changes, or there'll be hell to pay.'

'What's the third rule?' I asked.

'Third rule is, when nobody's watching, the cook gets to help himself. So you sit down here and try this soup while I get the water to boil. You'll be no use to me if you fall over dead from starvation, eh?'

He winked as he slopped a huge ladle of broth into a bowl and slid it along the bench towards me.

'Fourth rule is, never get caught!'

4.
Cygnet

I'm ashamed to say I slept like a dog for the rest of that dreadful night. Cook threw a square of tarpaulin under the galley bench to make a bed, and I curled up on it in a tight knot. The next thing I knew was a huge crashing of tin plates above my head as Cook dished out another meal at dawn. He'd left me to sleep through all the noise of a change in the watch, and when I crawled out from under the bench, he winked and waved me back to my bed.

Once the night watch had finished its food, there was a lull in the clamour of bare feet on boards and muttering tired men. Cook hummed to himself as he went about his work, and after the last sailor had gone to his hammock, he called out to me.

'Up you get, my little cygnet. Let's be seeing to that head of yours.'

I was a little unsteady on my feet as I stood up. The ship was well under way now, and there was a movement like the earth shifting back and forth below us. It didn't feel anything like the fine streaming motion of a little yacht on a steady swell or even in a bit of a chop. For all its size, this ship bucked, heaved and swayed against each wave.

'Steady on, girl,' said Cook. 'We've got a bit of weather up top and the captain's piling on the canvas. He loves a bit of a blow-up.'

He sat me down on a trunk and brought a bowl of steaming water. One glance at the gash on my head had him clucking and clicking his tongue.

'Dearie me, it's a nasty hole in your noggin you've got there.'

I touched my hair, all matted with dried blood and salt. It didn't hurt any more. Nothing did. I felt numb all through, except for my belly, which I don't mind admitting was feeling a little queasy.

But as he dabbed away at the blood and muck, every touch brought back the pain of the night before.

'Now then, now then,' Cook muttered, half to himself. 'What's the point of bashing my galley help? No brains, sometimes, those boys. You wait till I see that Jemmy. He'll be hearing from me, I don't care who knows of it.'

Every lurch of the ship took me further from home. I tried hard not to cry. I remembered all those long summer afternoons when I'd wished myself leagues away from that hot rock of an island, when I'd dreamed of a fast boat and a compass so I could sail towards the horizon and find adventure. Well, one night's adventure was about enough for any girl, if it was like this. Now I just wanted to be home. I imagined Mama waking beside the cold remains of the fire, calling my name. She'd wander the island all day looking for me, run down to town to call out the guards — she'd never give up on me, like she'd never given up hope for my father. But the thought of her sorrow was more than I could bear.

Cook patted my shoulder.

'There you go, lass. You'd best get to work now. Carlo will show you the water barrels and the salt pork. There's flour in the store, and I keeps all the potatoes down below out of the rain. There'll be no fish caught in this weather, so we'll make do with stew again. Captain won't be happy, but that's what he gets when he won't go into port except to blow things up. When I think of the raisins I could have bought in Santa Lucia. And fresh bread. Not even allowed to set foot on shore. Waste, that's what it is. What will become of us all? I don't know, really I don't.'

Santa Lucia. I cleared my throat.

'Pardon me, Cook, but why were you blowing up the town?'

'Don't ask me, lass. Captain don't tell me his plans, and I don't want to know 'em. But we lost four men sitting like ducks in a pond under those cannons up in the fort, and we got nothing to show for it but you.'

'It doesn't make any sense.'

'Not to you and me, girlie, but as long as it makes sense to Diablo, that's what matters.'

'Don't you care what he does? How many people he blows up?'

'It's nothing to a cook what captain we sail under. When I was younger I cared. Pride of the fleet, me. Gunner number two I was, sailed with admirals and all sorts. But nowadays I stay down below and keeps out of trouble. I don't have to do his devil's work, I just have to feed those that do. If they can sleep at night, well, so can I. Now stop worrying about things that aren't any of your business and go find Carlo.'

Funny thing is, as I left the galley, I felt scared. The cook, grumbling in the glow of his fires and steaming pots, was like a safe haven in this strange world.

'Stay out of the captain's wake!' Cook shouted after me.

No need to tell me that. I'd happily never lay eyes on Diablo again.

It was dark below deck, even in the light of morning. The hatches were slammed shut against the sea spray. From up above came the whine of the ropes in the wind and the cracking of canvas under strain, merging with the roar of white water along the hull. From the bow came the noise of hammering, as the carpenters repaired the damage done by the garrison guns.

Four pirates dead, and for what? To cover the raiding party that had found me alone on a moonlit track, I guessed. But what were they after? What was in that mysterious heavy package that had been dumped on the deck alongside one half-drowned girl in the middle of the night?

Who knew? Not me, and certainly not Cook.

I staggered along the narrow passage towards the stern. The boards seemed to be moving under my feet, and the walls swayed from side to side with the swell. I ducked down a trapdoor to find the water barrels lashed tightly together in the hold. Stinking green sea water sloshed below them. There was a damp smell of rotting wood and old beer. As I peered about me, with no idea what to do next, I heard feet clatter lightly on the steps above my head.

'*Merħba*,' said Carlo. 'Hello. How's your head?'

I shrugged. 'It's all right. Cook said you would show me where to find everything.'

'Of course. Follow me.'

'Where are you from?' I asked, as we squeezed past the water barrels, our backs pressed against the slimy ribs of the ship. 'What language was that?'

'I was speaking English.'

'No, there was another word — I didn't know what it was.'

'It's possible,' he said lightly. 'I speak so many languages — who can tell? My father is Portuguese, and my mother is Maltese. I speak four languages, you know, all without a trace of an accent.'

'Who told you that?'

'It is clear.'

'But you have an accent now, speaking English.' I couldn't quite place it. In Santa Lucia, our little harbour on the cross-currents of the world, I had heard so many different tongues that they all seemed to mingle together.

'Impossible. I am Carlo St Angelo de Santiago.' Somehow he managed to stand upright as he said it, in spite of the cramped hold.

'Sorry?'

'De Santiago is one of the great names of Malta. Surely you have heard of it.'

'Afraid not. I've never been as far as Malta. Is

that why your ransom is so high? Are you a duke or something?'

He looked a little crestfallen.

'No, I am not a duke. I will never be a duke. My half-brother inherits the title, but I . . . nothing. I am the younger son.'

He shoved his shoulder against a door to open it. Inside were more barrels, smaller and with tiny taps, a few stoneware flagons, and up higher a rack of dried meat.

'This is Cook's store. The men think it's locked, of course, but there's no key. Don't tell anyone.'

I shook my head. 'Aren't you afraid of these men at all, Carlo?'

'I am never frightened.'

'You'll make a good pirate, then.'

Carlo smiled, his teeth gleaming white in the gloom. 'Do you think so? I wish to be very fearsome.'

I smiled too, but I hoped he couldn't see me in the dark. 'Let's get this pork up to the galley, eh?'

'Cygno,' he said as we hauled a joint of meat up the narrow ladder, 'I don't really have an accent, do I?'

It was days before I saw Jem again, dark days of bad weather and endless battering by the waves. My stomach heaved many a time, until finally I got used to the movement and the wind died down and the ship slowed its hectic course. I got used to Cookie, too, with all his mutterings, and he became accustomed to finding me in his galley each morning.

'What did I do to deserve a girl under my feet day and night?' he'd bellow. 'Hell's teeth! Now, fetch me that vinegar and quick about it.'

One gloomy day we sat with our heads close together, sewing in the dim light that straggled down through the skylight above us. Cook clucked over my ragged clothes, and had managed to find, from a dead man's locker, a few bits and pieces that could be made to fit. He cut up an old jacket of his own that he would never be able to wear again — it probably hadn't fit around him for many years, but it hung all the way down to my knees.

'It'll last you for years, that coat, through storm and gale,' Cook said proudly, 'and we'll make a cap to match.'

The thick blue tarpaulin was as tough as sails to sew, and he showed me how to use the sail-maker's leather palm to protect my hand from the needle. I shortened the sleeves of a faded blue-and-white checked shirt. The canvas breeches were twice as long as I needed, and we turned the offcuts into a satchel I could sling over my shoulder.

'Don't go growing too tall, though, or your breeches will turn into pantaloons,' said Cook.

'They're not very clean,' complained Carlo, who was leaning against the wall, looking bored and hoping for something to eat. He was fussy about his own clothing, although it was starting to get a little tattered around the edges.

'They'll scrub up all right,' I said.

'More than I can say for some,' grumbled Cook. 'You, boy, look at the lace on your shirt.'

Carlo grimaced. 'I cannot help it. The lace tears so easily.'

'Beautiful shirt like that, no wonder. See how fine the linen is, Cyg? That shirt's not made for life on board a ship. Come here, lad, and I'll teach you how to mend it.'

Carlo's face betrayed his horror. 'Sewing is for womenfolk.'

'Like me, you mean?' I asked.

'Like me, he means, I guess.' Cook nudged me and chortled. 'Or any of the boys. We all sew, lad. Sailors have to know how to mend stuff. No womenfolk around. If you want to be a pirate, then you have to learn to darn and turn a seam.'

'Really?'

Cook patted the seat beside him. 'Come along, it won't kill you. Besides, it's nice and warm in here and there's pudding on the stove.'

Carlo reluctantly plonked himself down on the bench, looking for all the world like he was in dreadful peril.

The crew came in, one by one, cold and miserable. I knew them all now — Moggia, with his curly black hair, fat gold earring, and the devil in his grin; old Brasher, the toothless sail-maker, and his mate, Max; Ricardo, with four teeth and a red scar across one ear; his brother, Francesco, with the bright green eyes; and Harry, who rarely spoke. There were dozens more, from many parts, speaking many different languages. They all nodded hello to Cook, stared at me for a while, joked around, unless they were too tired, and went away to wolf down their meals in the crew's quarters. Big Miller, the bosun's mate, teased Cook about me every day.

'Behavin' herself, is she, Cookie?'

'As can be expected,' Cook would grumble.

'Yell if you need me to throw 'er overboard,' Miller would say, and laugh every time. After a while, I knew he didn't mean it. Mostly.

Jem had been taking his meals on deck, I guessed, riding out the storm with a few of the men who were hand-picked to sail *Gisella* in heavy weather. Late one night he appeared in the galley, rain streaming from his long hair.

'Got any coffee?'

The water was boiling on the fire, so I ground up some of the precious coffee beans and poured him a mug. He wrapped his bony hands around it and moved closer to the fire, nodding to Cook, who was crouched over a mound of half-rotten cabbages.

'Gale's dropped,' said Jem.

'Will we be docking anywhere soon?' asked Cook. 'Supplies is running mighty low.'

'You'll be sniffing Africa any day now.'

I sat up. Africa. Had we come so far?

Jem stared at me for a moment. 'How's your head?' Cheeky fellow.

'It's all right.'

'No need for you to go belting her over the conk like that, anyhow,' said Cook.

Jem snorted. 'Weren't me, although I should have clobbered her for lying.'

'Trying to save her own skin,' said Cook. 'Can't blame her for that.'

'Aye. Still, she don't seem like she suffered too much.' A smile danced in Jem's eyes. 'I wouldn't worry about that one, Cookie. You shoulda seen her dump Harry in the drink.'

Cook laughed his rare, wheezy laugh.

'Atta girl, that's my Cygnet.'

I giggled, but Jem's smile had vanished.

'What did you call her?'

'Cygnet,' said Cook. 'Although Carlo says it different, like, in Portuguese or something. It's a little —'

'I know what it is,' said Jem, roughly. He turned to me. 'I told you to keep that quiet.'

'I . . . I'm sorry. Cook asked my name and it . . . just came out.' I was stammering, suddenly afraid all over again. 'I told him I'd never heard of Rafe Swann.'

'So she did,' said Cookie. 'But I guessed she was romancing the truth a little. Relative or something, was he?'

I hung my head. 'He was my father.'

The men exchanged glances.

'S'alright, Jem,' said Cook. 'We just call her that for fun. Nobody else knows what it means.'

'They don't mean any harm by it,' I said.

'It's not me you need to fear,' Jem said quietly.

'No,' shouted a deep voice from the passageway.

'It's me you must fear!'

5.
The Blackbeard of Barbary

El Capitán de Diablo was leaning heavily against the doorframe.

'Fear me! The Blackbeard of Barbary!'

He laughed, way down in his throat. In his right hand was a sword, a jagged-edged boarding cutlass. His other hand groped for something to support him. He was as drunk as a toadfish, I could see. He had no hat on, just a red scarf wound around his head, with another at his·waist. His coat was wet through.

Jem and Cook just stayed quietly where they were, not moving. I did the same.

'Who's afraid?' Diablo yelled. 'Aye, you should all be afraid of me, every damn one of you!'

His fist slammed the wood above his head so hard that the candles spluttered in their lanterns. He glanced up, as if surprised to find himself below deck, instead of out in the open under a stormy sky.

'Well, I'll be blowed.' He seemed to be talking to himself, but his gaze suddenly fixed on me.

'Who the blazes is this?' he shouted.

At last, Jem took a step forward.

'It's the Santa Lucia girl, Cap. You remember, you banished her to the galley to help Cook.'

Diablo cocked his head to one side, trying to remember my face, perhaps even my arrival on the ship. His eyes were wavering, switching from me to Jem to the floor. Finally he banged his fist again on the beam above him.

'Damn right! Banish her to the galley. About bloody time!'

Jem took another step closer to his captain.

'We'd best get back up on deck, sir,' he said. 'We should be sighting the coast soon enough.'

Diablo sneered, a broad gape of rotten teeth through his beard.

'Tripoli, at last. Of course. Up on deck. Land ho! Where away?'

'On the larboard bow, sir, any time now,' Jem assured him.

'Tripoli and booty, beauty and booty, that's the course.'

'Aye, sir.'

Diablo spun around and staggered back towards the companionway. At the bottom of the ladder he stopped, put one foot on the lowest step, and then slumped downwards. Cook and I watched from the galley as Jem wrapped the captain's arm about his shoulders and dragged him to the cabin.

That night the fearsome El Capitán de Diablo went to bed early.

By the time he was on deck the next morning, the sun was well up and we were lying at anchor in a broad bay, circled by a sandy beach. The storm seemed to have blown itself out and blown us up onto the coast of Africa. It wasn't Tripoli. It wasn't anywhere, as far as I could see. There was no sign of life on the shore, only a couple of deserted huts on the beach, and the ruins of an old Roman theatre up on the crumbling cliff. Still, the captain looked pleased enough as he surveyed the coastline.

'Fine bit of navigating, if I do say so myself.'

'What do we do now, sir?' asked Jem, who was standing nearby. 'Any orders?'

Diablo peered intently at the horizon. 'No orders. We just wait. I'll be in my cabin. Call me if you sight a sail.'

'Aye, sir.'

Once the captain had stomped off below, I tiptoed up to Jem.

'Why are we hove to? Expecting another storm?'

'No, lass, we're expecting guests.'

'Out here? There's nobody about.'

'There will be, soon enough. Never you mind now. Cook'll be needing you down below, we've extra mouths to feed tonight.'

I scrambled down to the galley.

'Cookie! Jem says we're to have guests to supper.'

'Aye, so I heard.'

'Who is it?' I asked.

'I don't know and I don't care, and neither should you if you know what's best. All I do know is I've been told to cook no pork.'

'What?'

'Not allowed no pork, our guests.'

It took a moment to sink in.

'Jews? Are there Jewish pirates?'

'Course there are. There's all sorts. But tonight's guests? Arabs maybe. Who knows? Anyhow, we'd best get on with it. Tell Miller I need the last of the goats brought down. That'll have to do, though where we'll get another goat in these parts is a mystery to me.'

He clucked his tongue a few times and busied himself with a sack of vegetables.

'Quick about it, girl! And I'll need some chickens.'

We'd never had a feast on board *Gisella*, and just as well, too. It was hard work. Cook roped several of the starboard watch into rowing him to the beach to slaughter the goat and set it turning on a spit over hot coals.

I stayed on board, way below, scraping vegetables and baking flat bread. It was a terribly hot day, with no breeze to speak of. Whoever was coming to dinner was probably becalmed somewhere east of us. I didn't mind. If they didn't turn up, we'd have a roast goat and a mountain of food all to ourselves.

There was some kind of commotion on deck. I guessed it was Cook returning with the meat, and scrambled up the ladder to help ferry it aboard. There'd be plenty of sailors happy to carry it for him, but we'd never see that goat again if they got their greasy hands on it. But it wasn't Cook in his little rowing boat — it was another ship coming in to anchor in the cove beside us. A beauty she was, too, slender and sleek with one enormous blue sail and long oars arranged on either side. She was a glossy red, with a great blue and yellow eye painted on her prow.

Moggia was at the rails, watching closely. I stood beside him, both of us gazing in wonder at the ship and the men aboard her.

'Is it a slave galley?'

'No, no, she's crewed by freemen, I think, by the look,' said Moggia, 'She's a *taridha* — faster and smaller than a galley, and easier to handle in and out of these tricky little bays.'

'Are they from Algiers?' I asked. I didn't think I'd ever seen such men. Many were bare-chested like our crew, but several wore flowing blue robes, as light as a pennant in the breeze.

'Moors, I'd say. See those scimitars? Mighty swords, eh? Don't want to get on the wrong end of one of those, Cyg.'

'They'd slice you in two.'

'*Si*.' Moggia touched my shoulder. 'You slip out of sight now. Our guests aren't used to seeing a *signorina* on board ship. Stay down below with Cookie until they're gone.'

I nodded. There was something about these men, this strange meeting in the deserted inlet, which made me feel uneasy. I'd stay right out of harm's way.

There was enough to do, anyway. Cook returned with the roasted meats, shouting out for me to bring a cheese from the locker. Sweat ran in trickles down the backs of my legs as I stood over the boiling pans checking the puddings. It was as hot as Hades in the galley, but I felt safer there than anywhere on the ship.

Slowly the food disappeared, the fancy plates to the cabin where Diablo entertained the corsair captain, and great platters of meat up to the deck where the crews were sharing a gallon or two of Madeira. There was muffled music and sounds of stomping above us on the deck as the men started up a drunken jig or two, and from somewhere across the water the high note of a flute.

'Not so pure, after all, these Turks, eh?' Cook winked.

We were both exhausted, collapsed near the water pump — the coolest place in our little world. Cook chewed noisily on the goat's shin bone.

'Ah well,' he said. 'Pirates is pirates. They'll all be drunk before night, and then there'll be strife, you mark my words. No love lost between those two, you know.'

'Who? The captains?'

'Aye. Them barbarians is not popular with our captain, no sir.'

'I thought you said they were Turks.'

'Ottoman fleet's made up of all sorts. All heathens, if you ask me. World's never been the same since we lost the Crusades.'

'They certainly know how to sail. It's a beautiful ship.'

'Aye, fine crew, fine captain — I'll give 'em that.'

'Cookie, who are they?' I asked. 'There's no reason for them to be around here. They must be from Tripoli, surely. Or Tunis.'

'Whatever you say, young Cyg. You know better than I, as always.'

'But if Diablo hates them, why are we feeding them our last goat?' I asked.

'Who knows, lass? Who knows?'

'I'm sure you do.' I got to my tired feet and brought him a flagon of wine. 'You know everything that goes on aboard *Gisella*.'

He took another swig of wine. 'Maybe I do, but why would I tell you?'

'Don't, then. I don't care.' I moved towards the bench and started banging a few pots around. 'I'll scrub these, then we can get started on the salted fish.'

'No, no, it's too early. I just need some peace and bloody quiet.' Cook sighed and heaved his body further onto the bench. He settled into his story-telling face.

'You sit down and be good, for once, and I might tell you a tale.'

I brought a handful of figs, bartered from the corsair ship, and squeezed in beside him.

Cookie was in a talkative mood. Perhaps it was the wine. I waited for a long moment and asked, very softly, 'Tell me what you know about Rafe Swann . . . about my father.'

'Tall man, was he? Red beard?'

'I don't really remember,' I confessed.

'I do. Big red beard and wild hair to match. Not like your hair. Fiery red, it was. I saw him once in a tavern. Famous and feared, he was, Captain Swann.'

'That can't be him. My father wasn't captain of anything much.'

'Never mind then. I'll tell you a different story.'

'No, go on, please. You never know, it might be him.'

'Well, he and Diablo had a terrible fight.'

'Over what?' I asked.

'I don't know. This is before my time. Anyway, Diablo took Swann's ship — the *Black Swan*, I think it was.'

'That's wrong. He had a little fishing boat called the *Cygnet*, same as you call me.'

'Did he now? Ain't that a joke? Maybe it's a different man, after all. This Captain Swann had a captured French schooner. Only eight guns, but fast. She used to winter in Valletta Harbour. She was fine, sleek — aye, the *Black Swan*, she was. Feared all along the Barbary Coast, and Greece too.'

My heart fell through my belly fast as an anchor. All this time I'd hoped Cookie knew the truth, but the Rafe Swann he knew was someone completely different.

'So Diablo sank his ship — terrible fight it was, almost everyone killed and both ships shot to pieces. They marooned Swann on a rock somewhere. No one's heard of him since. Might be still there, poor soul.'

He stopped suddenly as Carlo ran towards us down the passageway.

'What is it, lad?' Cook called. 'They can't be wanting more supper.'

Carlo shook his head. 'No, they want Cyg.'

Me? A sudden flash of fear prickled across my scalp and down my neck.

'What do they want with her?' said Cook. He stood, towering over Carlo. 'They'll not lay a hand on my Cygnet.'

'I don't know. "Fetch the girl", that's all they said.'

'Are they drunk?' said Cook, gruffly.

'They don't appear to be. The Ottoman captain, he doesn't touch a drop.'

'Hmm. Well, all right then. But you tell the captain I need her back here, in one piece, to help with the pots.'

Carlo nodded.

'I don't really want to,' I said.

'I don't suppose you do,' said Cook. 'Can't say I would neither, in your place. Still, you'd best go get it over with.'

I just stood there.

'Go on, then.' Cook shoved me towards the door. 'But behave yourself. Don't argue with anyone. There's not many girls in this world who would argue with two pirate captains, but I wouldn't put it past you. So be nice, or I'll give you a clip across the ear.'

My shoulders slumped as Carlo took my arm and led me towards the cabin. Facing Diablo again was bad enough, but two of them? What could they want with me? Whatever it was, it wouldn't be good.

I tried to speak to Carlo, but there was nothing to say. He gave me a weak smile as he opened the cabin door and showed me in.

It was dark inside, and hellishly hot. Candles burned in the middle of a table strewn with bits of cake, parchment and a vast chart. The room was silent, but for the sounds of the ship's cat crunching chicken bones in the corner. I kept my eyes cast down.

'Here it is, our little flotsam,' said Diablo. 'Come in, and quick about it.'

'Aye, sir,' I whispered.

In the corner of the room was someone else, someone in pale blue, someone staring. At me.

'Come closer,' Diablo said, and I jumped a little at the sound.

I took two steps forward until my hands were nearly touching the table.

'Do you know Isola di Bravo?' Diablo asked.

It was such a simple unexpected question that I looked up, straight into his eyes.

'Off Santa Lucia?' I asked. 'Of course. My brother and I used to sail there.'

'Into the grotto?'

'Yes.' My voice was normal now, although I felt weak with relief. They only wanted directions. 'Well, you don't sail into it, you row into the cave until you get to the Golden Grotto.'

'Have you dived there?'

'In the Golden Grotto?' I waited for his nod. 'No, sir. It's too dark. You can't see. Besides, there are killer eels down deep.'

He laughed. 'Who told you that — some superstitious sailor?'

'It's not funny, sir, it's true. Everyone knows it.'

Diablo slammed his hand on the table and turned to the man in the corner. 'You see what I have to put up with? I told you.'

The man in the corner spoke quietly, almost gently. 'Look at me, child,' he said.

I did. His face was in shadow, but I could see skin too pale for a corsair. Yet his robes were light and flowed like a dress, or a sheet draped casually across a bed. At his belt hung a mighty sword, the scabbard jewelled and curving. He dressed like an Arab, but spoke like an Englishman — perhaps a faint lilt, a touch of Irish.

'Do you know me?' he asked.

I shook my head.

'Good.'

He stood, as best he could in the low cabin, his arm resting on the back of a chair. I could see him better now. He had blue eyes, and a white cloth wrapped about his close-cropped head. Not a real corsair at all, then. An Irishman turned Turk.

'So you know all about the Golden Grotto. You could take El Capitán de Diablo there, if he wanted?'

The last thing on earth I wanted was Diablo anywhere near Santa Lucia, but I nodded.

'I could take a small boat, that's all. You couldn't take *Gisella* close in to those cliffs.'

'I see.' His lips twitched a little. 'Do you by any chance know the Lion Cave on Santa Lucia?'

I stared down at the map. 'No, sir, I'm sorry. There are so many caves.'

I felt him move near. He was watching me.

'Can you read the chart, girl?' he asked.

It was a chart of the whole area, from Santa Lucia to Malta and on to Sicily. The coast around the island, my island, was well-marked — not as clear as the maps we had at home, but clear enough. My finger rested on the tiny rock that was Isola di Bravo, just to the east of Santa Lucia. I could imagine its cliffs, the white water that meant you were too close in, the cavern that led to the Golden Grotto.

'Who in blazes taught you to read a chart?' said Diablo.

'I'm not sure, sir. I've always known how. My father must have taught me, I suppose, when I was too little to remember.'

'Bait!' he shouted. 'That's what you are! I should have thrown you overboard the moment I saw you. I knew it. You're bewitched. Girls can't read charts.'

'That's enough,' said the corsair. He leaned over the map. 'She's right. That's the cove. She can lead you to the grotto, and that's what you want. Who cares if she's bewitched?'

Diablo muttered something about breaking my neck.

The corsair raised his hand to still the complaints.

'Your father taught you well. Is he perhaps a naval captain on some ship of the line?'

'Ha!' Diablo chortled. 'If you'd seen her when she fell onto our deck, you'd have known she was no captain's daughter. Never seen such a poor bloody sight. All scraggly and in rags. Not worth ransoming. Not worth feeding, for that matter.'

He waved me away.

'Get back to the galley. I'm sick of the sight of you.'

'Wait.' The other man's voice was softer. He bent

down, his face close to mine. I could smell spiced tea and lemons on his breath. 'Who is your father?'

'My father is dead, sir. He was a fisherman. He drowned at sea.'

'Fishermen don't usually have need of charts.'

'I don't know about that, sir. All I know is, I can sail and read a chart and catch a feed, and nobody really taught me any of it, as I remember. I was very young when he died.'

'But you can read?' he probed.

'My mother taught me that, sir.'

'You see, Diablo? She has a mother. You might have ransomed her after all.'

'Her mother taught her to be bloody cheeky. Probably some Santa Lucia tart, that's all.'

Stay calm, I told myself. Keep that anger tight and cold.

But he knew, that corsair. He cast a quick glance at my clenched fists and turned away.

Then, in an instant, I knew the name of this Barbary captain. I drew the secret from somewhere deep within me: the whispered name of every mother's fear. Hussein Reis. The Irish Arab. The fair-haired captain turned Turk, they said, and grown rich on the slavery route. One of the so-called renegades — European sailors who sailed in the fleet of the Ottoman Empire. Hussein Reis, captor of innocents, pillager of fishing towns and cathedrals alike. He showed no pity, never dispensed the mercy of Allah.

What did Hussein Reis want with Santa Lucia?

I felt as if we were fixed in time, the three of us,

suspended in amber like insects, in that stifling cabin. I waited for an eternity while Diablo studied the chart once more and mumbled to himself.

Every so often he shot a question at me. How high was the cliff around Isola di Bravo? Could it be climbed? Was there a ledge inside the grotto? How could I be sure?

Hussein Reis stared out the cabin window, as if surveying the coast. He was still staring, unsurprised, when the cry came from above.

'Sail ho!'

'Hell!' cried Diablo, scrambling to his feet. 'Clear for action!' he shouted as he ran from the cabin. 'Weigh anchor!'

There was a huge commotion on deck. I stayed where I was. So did Hussein Reis. I didn't dare move until he did. Finally, he sighed. 'What's your name, child?'

His eyes caught a reflection from the water outside the window.

'It's Lily, sir.'

'Lily? And your father's name?'

I gulped. 'I don't really know, sir.'

He looked away again. 'I see. Well, Lily, it seems like we're in for a scrap here, so you get yourself somewhere safe.'

'Yes, sir.'

'Oh and . . . Lily?'

I said nothing.

'You are right. It's a fool's errand looking for treasure in the Golden Grotto. Don't tell Diablo that — it only makes him angry. Let him search in vain if he must. But remember, should you need to, you can dive as deep as you like in the grotto, and you will find safety.'

'Yes, sir.'

I bobbed a curtsy, as best I knew how, and backed out of the room. What an odd man.

The ship was in uproar, with men running everywhere and carpenters clearing for action while gun crews ran out the cannon. The galley was chaotic, as Cook tried to douse the fires and stow his gear all at once.

'That's all we need,' he moaned. 'One moment it's bleedin' dinner guests, and then it's a naval patrol.'

I helped him batten down until he ordered me away to check on the livestock. On deck, the captain's voice was getting louder and louder as the crew scrambled to get some sail up, anything to get us out of the cove and into clear water. The sleek Arab *taridha* was already beyond the headland, oars striking the water in unison, its vast lateen sail catching the light breeze. At the tiller was the slender figure of Hussein Reis, in his blue robes, one arm raised in farewell to *Gisella*.

On the horizon were three ships on the hunt, perhaps for us — Spanish or French navy. Had they even sighted our masts against the coast? I said a silent prayer that we might be caught, swiftly and with no mercy.

The crew had some sail aloft, although not enough to make us too visible. *Gisella* lurched suddenly as the wind caught the canvas, though the boys were still groaning at the capstan, straining to bring the anchor to the surface. At last, with a final push on the spokes, they had the anchor free of the water and ready to be lashed down.

Another cry from above: 'Rocks! Away on the bow!'

A few of the men up on the yards were shouting down to us and pointing. I ran to the rails. We were drifting far too close in for my liking, with not enough wind to bring us about and out of danger. Nasty sharp-edged rocks, they were, too, with the waves crashing against them. Even in a small boat it'd be a close shave.

There was panic in the men's voices. I guessed they'd rather take their chances with the navy ships than be crushed against the rocks, here on the edge of the desert. On this desolate coast nobody would find a shipwrecked crew. Nobody would save us.

'About ship!'

Jem jumped up on the quarterdeck, calling out.

'Ready about!'

Miller was at the wheel, using all his weight to bring the ship around.

'Helm's a-lee!' he cried.

The deck watch let go the staysail sheets and ran across to pull the headsail tight. I ran with them, joined the end of the line, and pulled on the sheet with all my might.

It wasn't much, but it was just enough to get us under way. *Gisella* lurched again, out into the bay, and we tacked carefully into open water. The crew worked like demons, desperate to get away from this damned cove. The huge square sails had to be angled around on their yards to catch the wind. We heaved so hard on the braces I thought my elbows might pop out of their sockets.

It was the same as being out in the *Swallow* with Lucas, really, except there were ten times as many sails and sheets, and the pulleys were about as big as my head. But the sounds were familiar, and the luffing of the canvas told the same story. I helped as best I could, anticipating Jem's calls and running to wherever I could be of most use. I knew, like he did, when it was time to tack again, when to get ready, when to squint up at the sails for those tell-tale signs.

We rounded the headland at last, catching the off-shore breeze, and it wasn't until we were running downwind along the coast that we relaxed. Hussein Reis and his low, fast *taridha* were already out of sight.

Jem strode past to check on the foresail, and patted my head as he passed.

'Good work, Cygnet,' he whispered. 'You must be a hell of a sailor.'

It was then I realised I had helped *Gisella* escape, not just from a sure disaster on the rocks, but also from the ships that might have rescued me. I had lost myself in a moment of excitement, of danger, and had strained every muscle alongside these blasted pirates to help them to safety. Was I crazy? I sat down on the hatch, suddenly exhausted and feeling strangely empty inside.

Diablo stood oblivious on the quarterdeck, his telescope fixed on the sails away to the east. It was clear they had not seen us. I could hear the captain chuckle.

There would be no rescue for me. I was stuck on *Gisella,* and at that moment it seemed like my own stupid fault.

6.
Cut and thrust

After dark, we changed course again. The men who had gathered in the galley for their gruel were moaning, as usual, Cook louder than any.

'Feels like we're not headed for Tripoli after all, mates,' said Harry, his mouth crammed full of left-over goat meat. 'Due north, it is. Jem says we're sailing back the way we came, now we've shaken off those Frenchies.'

'It'll be biscuit and salt beef soon, just like the Navy,' warned Cook. 'If I don't see a market town in the next week, there'll be scurvy and hell to pay.'

I was huddled on my bed under the bench. I knew where we were headed, sure enough — back towards Santa Lucia, to Isola di Bravo and the Golden Grotto. Only God, Diablo and Hussein Reis knew why. I'd take them there. I had no choice. But there'd be little chance of escape, I knew that. If we sailed in from the south, even in the ship's launch, there'd be no way of landing. The cliffs on that side of the island were a hundred feet high, and the currents made it impossible to get in close. If I tried to swim ashore, I'd be smashed on the rocks.

The only opening in the cliff was the way to the grotto, and once there, I would find no escape in the caverns. Yet if we sailed so close to home, surely there must be some way to get free.

It was no good trying to think it out. If I stayed any longer on this ship, I'd become a pirate, too. Like Carlo. It was happening to me already. Somehow I had to get home. I had to get back to Mama, where the world made some kind of sense.

But the going was slow. It seemed like a whole season's storms had blown us across the sea and then towards Africa, and now it was a real struggle beating back against the wind. The Maltese sailors called it the *grigal*, a nasty nor'easterly that tore along the tops of the waves and took summer away with it. The *grigal* had come early this season, they said. Nobody had ever seen it at this time of year. Maybe the famous captain was not so lucky after all, they said in hushed voices. Maybe we should have gone to Tripoli or even Tunis. What were we doing, they asked, struggling against the *grigal* when there were prizes to be had in the south?

Diablo, as always, kept to his cabin and spoke to no one, besides giving Jem the sailing orders. Each day they were the same: beat to the north, under as much canvas as she'd take. The sailing was tough work, the men becoming more exhausted and bitter by the hour.

There'd been no prizes since they'd taken *Gisella* herself, though she'd been a rich enough haul, Ricardo told me one evening.

'A Spanish brigantine, she was, just launched and

full of shot and gunpowder,' he said. They'd sold the officers and crew as slaves, keeping the wine for themselves.

'Now we have *bella Gisella*,' said Francesco. 'We thought we'd rule the Mediterranean. We would be kings! But no.' The Vella brothers shook their heads in unison.

'Two towns we attack,' said Ricardo, 'but is there anything to show for this? No. Only the boy as a hostage. And what a hostage! He is seasick and cries for his mother, and then he says he will be a pirate too.'

'Then we kidnap you, Cygno,' Francesco teased. 'This is a very important raid. For what is a ship without a galley hand?'

They laughed, but then Ricardo dropped his voice to a whisper.

'But what is a ship without a captain, eh? Diablo, he runs from any sail he sees. Why? He has a ship that can smash any other to pieces. Why does he run?'

Francesco motioned to his brother to be silent. Ricardo shook his head.

'I do not understand it. But now, we go backwards. Did we forget something? Perhaps we forgot our courage. Ha!'

'Enough, Ricardo,' Francesco warned. 'You have said too much. Good night, Cygno. *Bonswa*.'

He shoved his brother ahead of him, down the companionway to the crew's quarters below. They were still arguing, in whispers. I sat on deck for a while longer, watching the familiar stars and listening to the ropes straining against the wind.

'We'll be there in two days.' Jem's voice sounded from the dark, somewhere behind me. 'If we had a decent wind, we'd be there and back by now.'

'How long have you been standing there?' I asked, startled.

'Long enough.'

'Don't hold it against them, they don't mean anything by it.'

Jem slumped down beside me on the hatch.

'Don't worry,' he said. 'They're good sailors, those Vella boys. I've kept them out of trouble many a time. They sure grumble like sailors, though. Anyone'd think they'd been press-ganged.'

'Like me, you mean?'

'Aye, lass, like you.'

'What will happen?'

'To you? I can't say.'

'Diablo's taking us back to Santa Lucia. He wants me to lead you into the Golden Grotto.'

'I know.' Jem's voice was grave.

'Can I go home after that?'

'I shouldn't think so.'

I was silent for a moment.

'What does he want with the grotto? There's nothing there, I've been in dozens of times.'

Jem shrugged. 'I've no idea. Captain's a mysterious man, and that's how he likes it.'

'Diablo and his mysteries!' I spat the words. 'You must know some of it, Jem. How could he have known my father? Was it Diablo who sold him as a slave?'

He looked startled. 'A slave?'

'Do you know what happened?'

'Quiet,' he whispered. 'I won't speak of it on this ship.'

'But I must know.'

'You will, one day, but not now.'

So he did know, and one day I, too, would learn the truth.

'I'll wait,' I conceded. 'But Diablo — has he really stopped attacking ships? Is he running scared, like the boys say?'

'Keep your voice down,' Jem warned. 'No, he's not scared. He's got some plan or other a-hatching. But if a pretty prize sailed across our path right now, I'd bet you a dozen doubloons he'd be after it.'

I didn't know then how soon Jem's words would become truth.

The cry came at dawn, from the night watch peering through a murky sunrise. Two sails to starboard, downwind: a merchant ship with a smaller escort, probably a sloop. The men all thundered on deck to size them up.

'Ripe for the picking,' cried Miller from up in the tops. 'Greeks, I'd wager.'

'They've seen us, too,' said Max. 'Look! They're breaking out their topsails.'

Sure enough, in the distance, extra canvas billowed from the topmasts. They were hoisting as many sails as they could, trying to escape. At that moment, Diablo appeared on the quarterdeck. Every man stood still and waited for his word. He scrutinised the ships through the telescope for what seemed forever.

'Boys,' he said quietly, 'clear for action.'

A few of the men cheered, but they were drowned out by the tremendous shouting that suddenly rose on deck.

'Hoy there, clear for action!'

'Starboard watch, hands to the topsails!'

'Max! Run out the jib as well.'

This time I would not help them. I couldn't even watch as *Gisella* gained on her prey. I retreated down below, where Cook was in a frenzy packing up the galley in readiness for battle.

'There you are, girl. About time, too. Now you'll learn what it's all about.'

'I don't want to know anything more. I'm sick of this ship, and everyone on it.'

Cook stopped what he was doing and looked me straight in the eye.

'You listen here, princess. It may well be that you're sick of being here, but you aren't the only one.' He was glaring at me, hands on his hips, looking, despite his size, just like my mother when I was in really big trouble.

'We're about to go into action. You don't know what that is — you've never seen it. I'm not going to lock you up like young Carlo, because I need you to help me. You are about to learn the other half of being a ship's cook — buccaneering or naval, it's all the same. This galley is about to become a hospice, and you're going to be right here with me doing everything I tell you. Do you understand me?'

I nodded. I thought I understood.

'Right, get Carlo to bring up two barrels of water

and a cask of brandy. Then tell Miller to lock Carlo up out of the way. We don't want him damaged. He's precious goods.'

I nodded again and ran off, calling out for Carlo among all the shouting men amidships. The guns were being rolled and lashed into position with thick hawsers, and powder casks were dragged across the floor. Moggia was handing out cutlasses and boarding axes, shouting for everyone to save their blunderbuss shot until the last moment.

The ship was flying now, I could tell. Jem must have had her under every possible sail, close into the wind. There would be no stopping her.

I couldn't find Carlo anywhere. Cursing like an old tar, I grabbed Francesco and forced him to help me with the barrels. He lifted them up out of the hold easily, rolled them down to the galley in a few minutes, and ran off again, a strange, wild, fearful stare in his eyes. Everyone had the same air about them: scared and excited at the same time.

Jem stuck his head into the galley briefly, saw me there with Cook tearing up cloth for bandages, and nodded to us both.

'No sign of the boy?'

'Perhaps he's hidden himself,' Cook suggested.

'Hope so.'

Jem had a dagger in his belt and a cutlass in his hand. He seemed to be more gloomy than fearsome. I wanted to wish him good luck, but held my tongue. These men, most of them anyway, weren't bad men at heart. But their good fortune today would be another's ill luck. Some of them would die, perhaps under my hands in this dismal galley. Some of them would be terribly hurt.

But many others, perhaps, would die or be sold as slaves, like my father.

I stared at my hands. They were trembling.

When I looked up, Jem had gone. A quiet had settled on the ship.

'What happens now?' I asked.

'It depends how much the other captain values his life, or his ship,' said Cook. 'If he has a high opinion of one or the other, he'll fight like a demon and so will we.' He sighed. 'Make no mistake, it's a terrible thing. Diablo's not a pretty sight in a fight. Something happens to him, something takes him over until his blood boils. He's like one of them Viking berserkers. There's no stopping him.'

My blood wasn't boiling; it was freezing in my veins. I could imagine Diablo mad with anger or bloodlust or greed — whatever it was, I wanted no part of it.

Carlo suddenly appeared in the galley door.

'Here you are at last,' cried Cook. 'Come along, we're to stow you below.'

'Not this time,' Carlo said. 'This time, I fight!'

'Don't be silly, boy. You'll get hurt and then where will we be?'

'You cannot stop me,' said Carlo. 'I am a man, not a boy, and I must fight, not cower below decks with cooks and girls.'

He sounded more scared than anything, but he brandished his sword theatrically. Everything Cook had said suddenly became dreadfully clear. I took

Carlo by both arms and pulled him close to me.

'Carlo, listen to me. People are about to get killed and maimed and God knows what else.'

'I don't care,' he said. 'I am not afraid.'

'You should be,' muttered Cook.

'Cookie's right,' I said. 'You are more likely to end up with your arm shot off or something horrible. A cannonball just minces people to bits. It is not glorious.'

'There is no glory hiding in the storeroom! I am ashamed. I am a son of Lorenzo de Santiago and I do not hide.'

'But these people are not your friends, Carlo. They would kill you if they didn't think you were worth money. They will probably kill me one day because I'm not worth anything. You can't fight for them. They're pirates. It would shame your family if you fight under a pirate flag.'

At this, he laughed, shaking himself free of me.

'Cygno, you know so little. I am a nobleman, yes. But I come from a long line of pirates. When I am sixteen, I will become a page to the Knights. One day I may be a captain of corsairs. I am, after all, Maltese.' He bowed, one hand on his chest.

'Excuse me. *Skużani.*'

Then he was gone.

At the same instant, a huge blast shattered the quiet. The battle had begun.

I heard later how it happened, how Jem took *Gisella* in between the two fleeing ships while our crew got ready to board, cutlasses in hand; how Diablo blasted his prey with a broadside from each side;

how the merchant ship, the richest prize, sank almost immediately, her gunpowder casks exploding in an inferno that nearly sank us all; how Diablo cursed, left the burned survivors to drown, and raced after the sloop.

By then, the first wounded were being brought to the galley. The sloop had got off a round from its twelve-pounder that had put a hole right through the bows of *Gisella* and taken off Harry's left arm. He was carried in screaming, and kept screaming while Cook tried to staunch the flow of blood with a wad of linen.

Old Brasher limped in with a piece of wood the size of a belaying-pin sticking out of his thigh. 'Pull that out for me, lass,' he said. 'I've got to be getting on. Captain's ready to board.'

I put both hands around the splintered wood and yanked as hard as I could. Brasher let out a mighty roar. 'Good girl,' he said, when he'd caught his breath. I tied up the wound as Cookie had taught me, and Brasher hobbled back to the action.

Harry was whimpering now, reciting some half-forgotten prayer. Cook stood by his side, just waiting. Harry was not long for this world.

It seemed we were all waiting. The ships collided with an enormous thud that threw me to the floor. A roar from above meant the crew was boarding the other ship, swords and daggers drawn. There was gunfire — muskets or boarding pistols, I couldn't tell — and shouted curses, stopped dead by a scream. More shouting, and then the clash of sword on sword. The din was terrifying, but seemed strangely muffled.

After a few minutes, Francesco dragged in a wounded man and dumped him in the middle of the floor.

'We have boarded,' he shouted, 'but they fight like demons!' He ran back to the fray.

Brasher staggered in again, this time with a sword gash across his forehead. I pushed him down onto the bench, and scolded. 'This time, you're staying here.'

I don't think he minded too much. There was blood on his cutlass.

'I gave as good as I got, you know, lass.'

'I'm sure you did,' I assured him.

'Cookie!' came a call down the hatch. 'Come quick.'

Cook didn't even glance up from the wound he was tending.

'You'll have to go, girl. I can't take my hands off this. Take some cloth and the brandy. But don't let the liquor out of your sight.'

I didn't move.

'Go!'

Of course. Someone was hurt. I scrambled up the ladder with the bottle in one hand, and emerged into bright sunlight. *Gisella*'s deck was empty. Ropes were strewn over the starboard rails, and I looked down over the side at a scene of mayhem.

The little sloop had been blasted by cannon, fouling the rigging and smashing the tiller. A tangle of shrouds and canvas lay across her stern and dipped into the sea. There was an odd group of men near the bow, wrestling and pushing each other like schoolboys, and the sound of swords clashing somewhere below decks.

All over the ship, men were lying in the strangest

positions, staring straight up into the sky, collapsed face down on the boards, or curled into corners, moaning. There was blood everywhere.

'Hey there, Cyg. Bring the swabs!'

Miller was crouched over someone near the mast. He waved to me, urgently. I tucked the linen and bottle into my shirt, threw myself over the side, and slipped down a rope to the deck of the captured ship. I ran over to see who was wounded.

It was Max, slumped over someone else's dead body. He had a hole through his blouse, and blood coursing down his side and onto the deck, where it mingled with other people's blood.

'What hit you?'

'A sword slash. Blasted thing. There were two of 'em at once, I couldn't take 'em both. Got 'em in the end, though.'

I peered at the gash in his side. It was clean, and the bleeding seemed to be slowing. 'Seems all right,' I announced, as if I'd been a surgeon all my life. 'I'll just wrap you up, and we'll get you back aboard *Gisella*.' It did seem all right, compared to Harry or any of those other poor souls lying all over the ship.

Miller ran off, cutlass in hand, to rejoin the attack.

I was tying the bandage at Max's waist, when there was a clash of swords quite near to us and Max cried out, 'Look out behind you!'

I spun around to see Carlo trapped in a strange embrace with a man in a blue uniform. Their swords were locked together, and they were both grimacing as they pushed each other backwards, first one way, then the next.

The soldier grunted, shook himself free, and landed Carlo a thump on the head with his sword pommel. That decked him. His face went white and he dropped like a sinker. The soldier stepped quickly over Carlo and raised his sword. Above me.

'No!' I shouted.

I pushed Max to one side and rolled to the other. The sword came down on the deck between us with a thwack. I kicked out at the soldier's knees, hitting him hard and knocking him off balance. As he steadied himself, I reached for Carlo's sword and scrambled to my feet.

The blue-coat turned to face me. Everything I knew about sword-fighting, every thrust and parry Flynn had taught me on those hot afternoons in the *piazza*, seemed to vanish from my mind in an instant. I drew the sword up before me. We were standing close, a sword's length apart, face to face. He smiled.

'*Mademoiselle*,' he said, bowing ever so slightly. I didn't take my eyes off him.

He lunged, so fast I only just blocked it in time. He was strong, far stronger than the boys in Santa Lucia. A few more blows like that, and I wouldn't be able to hold him. But I was fighting for my life. Before, I had only fought for fun.

I watched him. He was scared, twitching his coat nervously with his left hand. Another breath, and he'd try again. Now! A slash towards my head, parried high across my face, then another, weaker, thrust down low. I smacked it away hard. There! His arms were longer than mine. I had to keep out of his reach.

But he wasn't thinking clearly. I took a quick step

forward and feinted, the point of my blade flickering close to his shoulder. He panicked and stepped back. I could see he wasn't prepared for this. He blinked. I lunged, fast, aiming just above his hand. He saw me coming, jerked his guard up. My blade circled his and slid under his fist, then I lunged again. I felt the tip of my sword jar on something. A belt, I hoped, not a bone.

I heard Miller shout from somewhere, 'Look at Cyg!'

I took a step back. The soldier did, too. Then, ever so slowly, he crumpled to the boards. Blood gushed from a wound in his thigh.

I'd done that. I had stabbed a man.

Jem was beside me now, his blade pointed at the throat of my foe.

'Leave him,' I said. The soldier was not dead. He was weeping.

Jem didn't move.

'Jem,' I said, 'is it all over?'

At last he took the point of his sword from the man's throat. 'Aye, lass. The captain's still down below raising hell, but the ship's ours.'

'I'll get back to the galley. Have them bring the wounded up.' Suddenly I was very tired.

The sword dropped from my hand.

Jem nodded. 'I will.'

Slowly I reached down and grasped the sleeve of the blue uniform. The soldier gazed up through bleary eyes.

'Come on, then,' I said, pulling him up. 'Let's be getting you patched up.'

7.
The flying *Mermaid*

For days the two ships drifted, roped together, in a sluggish sea. We all worked like slaves to repair the damage and keep both afloat. The men worked on the beams and ropes, while Cook and I worked on the men.

At first we just patched them up as best we could. Time was the best surgeon, said Cook, and he was right in a way. Harry died on the first night, and his body was thrown, with the other dead, over the side. Nobody said a prayer for him or anyone else. There was no time. Diablo drove us like a madman, stomping around the deck of the big ship, shouting down at the crew toiling under the hot sun on the sloop.

The men called her the *Mermaid*, and she had been fresh out of Alexandria, making for Algiers, when she had stumbled across our path. I watched as her surviving crew members were shackled. Mostly poor Egyptians, they pleaded for mercy. But there were soldiers, too, in blue coats, like the one I'd fought. French, I guessed, but what they were doing out here on an Ottoman ship, we couldn't say. Perhaps they had no idea themselves. Their officers were all dead, and the ship's captain, I heard, had shot himself rather than be taken prisoner. The soldiers and captured crew, even the wounded, were herded into *Gisella*'s fetid hold.

Late on the second day, a bell sounded and all hands were called onto the deck of *Gisella*.

'All hands,' shouted Carlo as he ran past the galley. 'That means you and me, too!'

On the quarterdeck, El Capitán de Diablo stood with his sword in his hand, glaring out at the crew gathered below him. There was a bit of pushing and shoving as men tried to get into the front rows. Cook and I stood at the back.

Jem was standing behind the captain, a few feet away, not looking at us but across into the still-tangled rigging of the *Mermaid*. He seemed to be wishing himself leagues away.

Diablo banged his sword pommel on the mast to get some quiet.

'We have a prize!' he shouted, and there was a ragged cheer from the men. Too many remembered that the real prize, the merchant ship, had gone to the bottom. The little *Mermaid* was not much consolation.

'This prize is worth maybe two thousand *scudi* in port, to some enterprising merchant in need of a fast ship. And let's not forget our young duke, whose father waits so impatiently for his beloved son's return that the ransom money will be burning a hole in his purse.' He pointed his cutlass at Carlo, who blushed.

'So we need a crew to sail the prize ship to Valletta to be sold, collect our ransom for the boy, and wait there for *Gisella* to return.'

The men were silent. They waited to see what their choices might be. There was no point in volunteering if it meant missing out on more prizes.

But Diablo wasn't asking for volunteers. 'All the wounded will go to Valletta,' he announced. 'Those who can no longer fight will be discharged there. I have made a list of the others who will sail the *Mermaid*. Jem McGuire will be in charge of the prize crew.'

The men glanced at each other. This wasn't the pirate way — even in the navy, sailors would be given the chance to volunteer. But no one spoke. Not yet.

Diablo went on, shouting above our heads in his coarse, gravelly voice. '*Gisella* will set course tonight for Algiers. I find I have business there that cannot be delayed. I will take the captives with me.'

Not Isola di Bravo. Nowhere near Santa Lucia. *Gisella* was heading back to Africa, further from my home and further from freedom.

The crew was as disappointed as I was. 'Hey, Captain, we've had enough of your business,' one man shouted, from the safety of the huddle. 'We want more prizes!'

'*Iva!*' shouted Ricardo and Francesco in unison.

Miller shuffled forward through the pack. 'That's enough, boys,' he muttered. He lifted his face to the quarterdeck. Jem raised a hand to hush him, but he kept on. 'But fair's fair, sir. It's months since we've had any real action. How's about we sail in convoy for a few weeks, see what we can pick up, and then sell off the sloop? She seems a fair sort of ship.'

Diablo glared down at Miller, and then his gaze

wandered over the faces of all the crew. I shivered.

'Algiers,' spat one of the Sicilians. 'There is nothing but pox and sand in Algiers.'

'Who said that?' Diablo roared. He brandished his sword above his head.

None of us moved. The captain moved slowly and quietly down the steps and onto the deck. Without speaking, he circled the crew, staring into their faces. Each man quailed under his glare. One by one, they cast down their eyes, clasped their hands before their bellies, and hoped he would not take his revenge on them. At last, Diablo came to a halt next to the Sicilian. He did not look at him. When he spoke, it was in a whisper.

'Who said that?'

There was no answer.

Like a sudden squall, Diablo lashed out at the Sicilian, slashing at him with his cutlass and thumping him to the ground with hard, thwacking punches. The Sicilian raised his hands before his face, crying out for mercy, for the Holy Mother to save him.

'No one will save you,' Diablo screamed. 'You parrot-fish! You question me? Who dares to question me?'

The Sicilian lay slumped on the deck, his face badly cut and his hands clasping a bloody wound in his side.

'You!' Diablo grabbed another man. 'Throw him over the side!'

It took only a moment for the man to react, but it was too slow for Diablo. Again he lashed out, striking a blow on the sailor's arm so hard that he, too, fell to the boards.

Diablo spun around, facing the rest of the crew. 'Any more questions?' he shouted. 'Good. I'll be in my cabin. McGuire, you have your orders. Get your crew on board the sloop and be out of my sight before sunset.'

There was silence as he pushed through the crowd and disappeared below. The men stood and stared at each other in disbelief. No one went to help the two wounded men, in case the captain's wrath was a disease that could be passed on.

'Let's get them below,' Cook murmured in my ear. He crouched down beside the Sicilian, but it was too late. One of Diablo's blows had severed a vein in his neck, and he was already dead. I tried not to look at him too closely. Cook picked up the other casualty as if he were a child.

'Come, lass, we'd be better off in the galley.'

'Not you, Cyg,' said Jem. 'You're coming with us.'

'On the *Mermaid*?' I hadn't dared hope for that.

'I don't think so!' Cook blustered, plonking the poor injured man down on a heap of ropes as if he were a sack of potatoes.

'I asked for a cook, and Diablo said I could take her,' said Jem, firmly. 'She'll have to work hard though, we're short-handed. You'll be crew as well as cook and galley hand, Cyg. It won't be easy.'

'I don't mind.'

My whole body felt lighter and cleaner than it had for weeks. I'd be free of Diablo, closer to home, sailing on the *Mermaid*. Valletta was a big city, so I'd heard. Easy enough to give them the slip and run off. Steal a boat, maybe. It was a few days' sail from Malta to

Santa Lucia, but I could do it. If I had to. If I was free.

But Cook had crossed his arms. 'Over my dead body.'

'Whatever you say.' Jem wasn't the sort of fellow to be put off by an irate cook. He just walked aft, calling over his shoulder, 'Lend us some spices as well, while you're at it, Cookie, I can't stomach that Egyptian mutton.'

'Well, I'll be dumblustered,' spluttered Cook. 'I never did hear of such a thing, not in all my born days.'

'It'll be all right, Cookie,' I assured him.

'Don't know what'll become of you, once you're out of my sight. Dearie me. Anything could happen.'

'I could be kidnapped or something.'

He never understood my jokes.

'Yes, anything!' he cried, bundling the injured man up in his arms again, and thumping his way down the ladder. I followed in his wake like whitebait.

In time he calmed down, and fretted over what I might need to take with me. I checked the galley on the *Mermaid*. It was just a fireplace amidships with a couple of cauldrons, but there was a good storeroom, and a hatch up above let the sunlight in. Cookie bundled up my bedding, a hammock, and a spare shirt.

'That'll have to do, I can't spare any more, what with no supplies and the chickens all dead in the heat.'

'We'll be right enough, Cookie.' I heard the bell up on deck. The *Mermaid* was ready to go.

'Oh dear,' Cook said one last time.

I felt an unexpected pang of sadness for this good man trapped in a ship with a tyrant. He'd been kind to me, when I'd anticipated something so much worse. I looked up to see a tear in his eye, and held his huge hand in both of mine for just a moment.

'Thank you for caring for me,' I said.

'No such thing,' he muttered.

'We'll meet again, Cookie, I know we will.'

He smiled down at me, and patted my hand.

'Aye, dearie, I believe we will, one day.'

As I walked away from him and climbed up onto the deck of *Gisella* for the last time, I could hear him muttering into his pots and pans. 'You're a silly old fool, Cookie. Crying over a child. What will become of you? I just don't know.'

Jem was at the helm of the *Mermaid* when I dropped from the rope, softly, on to the deck and made my way aft.

'Up the ratlines with you, girl, and get that halyard free,' he said. 'You're a sailor now. You know what to do.'

'I should put the galley to rights.'

'Plenty of time for that,' he said. 'We've got to put the ship to rights first.'

The towline was cast off, but it took an eternity for us to move out of the shadow of *Gisella*. We were slow at our work, tripping over unfamiliar ropes and flailing about until we got the feel of our new ship and crept away under only the headsail.

Amidst the shouts and the creaking, we could hear the jeers of the men aboard the brigantine. The forenoon watch stood along the rails and laughed, waving while we untangled the mainsail.

'Don't go sinking our prize, Jemmy, or you'll have my wife to answer to!'

'Oi! West is that way.'

'See you in Valletta, mates, if you don't feed the fishies on the way!'

Diablo waited grimly on his quarterdeck until we were under way before shouting orders to his remaining men. I risked one last glance up at him, as he scowled at the sunlight and wiped other people's blood from his cutlass.

'Last I'll see of you, Captain,' I muttered under my breath, 'this side of hell.'

I reached up to grab the shrouds. The tarred ratlines, well-spliced and taut, felt fine under my fingers and feet as I climbed. The mast was only half as high as *Gisella*'s topsail, and a clear light timber that glowed yellow in the sun. She'd be fast, this little sloop, handled right and sailed sweetly. The rigging was slippery as goose fat and tangled as guts after the fight, but the boys and I hung on like old salts and teased apart the web of rope. Finally, we let the sail loose in one sweet fall. It billowed, pale as cream, before the deck men pulled it tight.

The *Mermaid* leaped forward through the swell as if unleashed. We left *Gisella* in our wake. There was a whoop, then laughter from our deck.

As long as I live, I'll never forget those first days of sweeping across the ocean, wind swelling the sails, pushing her another knot or two. How fast could she go? We leaned with the breeze, logging nine knots, ten. Eleven! She was a sprite, a flying fish.

How she shone! We swept and swabbed and scrubbed away all traces of blood and fury, all the filth from below decks, all the gunpowder and shredded cloth. Jem put us to tarring the ropes, and mending some torn sails we found stuffed below in old canvas bags. We slept on deck, all of us, under the stars, and woke each morning in delight at the sails and the sun above us. Carlo and I spent a whole day washing down the galley and setting things straight in the cook's store.

We ate well, those days, breaking open drums of pork and salted beef. Diablo had been a little too hasty in casting us off with all the stores aboard. He'd been too keen to be rid of us, rid of the *Mermaid*, to bother ransacking the hold. Stashed below were great bags of dried apricots and plums, sacks of flour and sugar, vats of Madeira that Jem had locked away until we could reach safe harbour and celebrations. On the Sunday night, a day or so out from the Maltese coast, I fashioned a vast pudding of the kind only ever sighted in a captain's cabin.

We ate it together, all on deck, a spoon in each hand and a cup of fine wine to toast ourselves and our *Mermaid*. Nobody proposed a toast to Diablo.

We sat about under light sail after the wind had dropped, resting tired limbs and grinning at the stars. Miller broke the silence with a comment that would change our lives forever.

'You know what, boys? I don't want to sail to bloody Valletta.'

There was muted laughter of agreement, a few mumbled ayes.

I took a breath, and when I let it out, the strangest words emerged with the air. 'We don't have to,' I said.

They all looked at me. Jem sat up straight. Everything was suddenly quiet. Were they thinking me mad, or waiting for me to say something even worse? So I did.

'We don't have to do anything Diablo says any more.'

'That's mutiny, lass,' someone muttered.

'Not on this ship,' I said. 'He holds no sway here, unless we let him.'

'It's Diablo's prize, Cyg. You can't rob a captain of his booty!'

'It's our prize. We all risked our lives to take her, and we've made her a better ship than Diablo could ever dream of.'

'What are you saying, girl?' Jem asked me.

In for a penny, in for a pound, I thought.

'I'm saying this — we have a fast ship, a fine crew, eight good guns, and a few stores to trade. I say we're pirates enough to take on any ship in these waters. We should keep sailing until we're good and ready to go to Valletta.'

'You're talking rot,' said Miller. 'Pass the wine, there's a good girl.'

'No — listen to me. You saw the captain's face when he chose this prize crew. He didn't need to send so many of us. Some of you are his finest sailors.'

'He chose men he could trust,' Miller retorted.

'He was ridding himself of all his troublemakers before he sailed for Algiers.'

It was becoming clear to me as I spoke it aloud, although I didn't say what was really in my mind — Diablo had got rid of all those he thought were a bit soft-hearted to be proper cut-throats.

'He wanted us all off *Gisella* for good,' I went on. 'So I say we go find our own trouble.'

'I'm no troublemaker,' said Brasher. 'I've served under 'im all of five years, never given 'im a moment's grief.'

'You're right, Brasher,' I countered. 'Then why send you away, eh? You're wounded, but not so badly you have to be paid off.'

'I made trouble for him,' Ricardo piped up, 'and I'm not sorry for it.'

'You make trouble for everyone,' I teased. The boys laughed, and Francesco dug his elbow into his brother's ribs.

Jem smiled, just a little. He, at least, was listening carefully to me. I kept talking, fast.

'Miller spoke up against him, for sure. But Brasher? Jem? Moggia? He knows each one of you is as smart as he is. He just doesn't want anybody on *Gisella* arguing with him.'

'Now you sound like one of them Frenchie revolutionaries,' said Brasher.

'She's right about some of it, but not all,' Jem spoke up at last. 'There's another reason, by my figuring. Look at us. We're all Englishmen, Maltese, Sicilians, Irishmen. There's only Egyptians and Frenchmen left on *Gisella*.'

'Of course,' I shouted. Why hadn't I seen it before? 'He's going to make a pact with the Turks. That's why he met with Hussein Reis. Then he'll set a course . . . to the Adriatic, maybe. He means to join with Hussein and attack Christian ships!'

'He wouldn't,' said Moggia. 'Venice would send out fleets against him. You can't hide from them. They have spies in every port.'

'I don't think it's east he's sailing,' said Jem.

I glanced over at him. Perhaps he knew more than I realised. He guessed my thoughts and shook his head.

'Nobody in their right mind sails east searching for prizes in this season — the winds are too variable. No, I think it's Algiers, then Majorca or maybe Spain.'

'He's mad!' cried Moggia. 'The English fleet will come. Even *Gisella*'s no match for a ship of the line.'

'It could be either — it's no matter,' Miller said. 'Venice is old and weak. All of Europe is busy fighting the French. General Bonaparte is on the march. Nobody will care about one rogue pirate ship.'

Carlo smiled. 'Maybe Diablo is smarter than you think.'

'Maybe,' I conceded.

'He's not a man to be double-crossed, I know that,' said Miller. 'You think you can just sail off in his prize ship? He'll come after you, and I wouldn't like to see what happens then.'

'It'll be winter before he comes back, wherever he's gone, if he ever does,' I said. 'We could borrow the ship, if you like. Sail into Valletta, as ordered, but not tomorrow or the day after — just . . . eventually.' I even smiled at myself. It all sounded so simple.

'We could sail to the Levant for winter,' suggested

Ricardo, 'or set ourselves up nicely in Cyprus, some-where he'd never find us.'

'Or we could hang from his topmast,' warned Miller. 'I've seen 'im do it to plenty of men for much less a sin.'

'But that's what I mean.' I was on my feet now, breathing heavily. 'We don't need to live in fear of someone like that. It's not how pirates should live. I'm saying we do it the old way, all of us — share and share alike — vote on where we sail, who we're after, how much booty each man gets.'

'But who'd be captain? Ship's gotta have a captain,' said Brasher.

I looked around me. 'Jem's the best sailor amongst us. That's what a captain is. He can be sailing master, if you like, so when we're in a gale or after quarry there's one wise voice to shout the orders.'

'Aye,' someone murmured, 'makes sense.'

'I can sail a course, Cyg, but I can't figure one,' said Jem. 'I'm no navigator, wouldn't pretend to it.'

'I'll be your navigator, then,' I said. 'We'll stick to the coastlines we know, and I can set a course if there's need.'

'You?' Miller scoffed. 'You're a little young, don't you think?'

'I can chart a course and use the quadrant,' I retorted. 'Can you?'

He shook his head.

'As for the rest, we meet like this and decide together — the watches, the attack plans, any discipline.'

'No flogging?' asked Ricardo.

'Not unless we all vote yes.' They were with me now. I could feel it.

'There's one more problem,' said Miller.

We waited.

'We'll need a proper bloody cook if you're going to be turning yourself into a midshipman.'

The laughter was like music. We all shared the relief, and a few men even cheered.

'We'll just have to kidnap another cook.'

'That's another thing,' I ventured.

'Oh, what now? You want to be the quartermaster?'

I grinned. Everyone smiled with me.

'We've lost fifteen men in the last two attacks.'

Heads bowed. I went on.

'It makes me wonder: if you're a trader captain, and you see a pirate ship bearing down on you, why not just surrender? Why fight to the death, when you know you'll be beaten, your ship ruined and all your men slaughtered? It's not just honour, and they can't all be fools. When we sank that merchant ship, Cookie made me realise why — it's the fear of being sold as slaves. It's not losing the ship or the loot that matters to them. Given the choice between a life of slavery or death in battle, what would you choose?'

The Vella brothers exchanged glances.

'No, lads, taking slaves makes our life twice as hard as it needs to be,' I said. 'First, you have to fight like demons to take the ship — look at us — all those men dead and plenty wounded beyond repair. Then you have to keep the people alive, and sail clear across the sea to be rid of 'em. It just doesn't make sense.'

'Take no prisoners?' said Jem. 'You mean, kill 'em all?'

'That's not it. I had something more radical in mind. We should let them go free.'

That really got them laughing.

'I mean it,' I shouted above the din.

'You're crazy, girl.'

'Some of 'em we might not let go without a pretty ransom, of course,' I said.

'Now she's talkin' sense.'

'But ransom or no, we take them into port and drop 'em off safe and sound.'

'You've gone daft, Cyg,' said Miller. 'Pirates don't do that. We're killers. Remember? Pillagers. Cut-throats. We're supposed to strike fear into the hearts of every living being.'

'One look at your face, Milly, and they'd fall down dead,' shouted Francesco.

'I know about fear, Miller.' My voice dropped down low, and they all leaned in a little closer. 'I've been a slave. I've lived in fear of all of you. You were supposed to kill me. But you didn't. You took pity on me and here I still stand today. You're no cut-throat, Ulysses Miller, and I'm the proof.'

'Aye, Milly, you should have finished her off when you had the chance.' Jem punched him on the shoulder. 'Now we're stuck with her and she won't shut up.'

I wouldn't shut up, not now.

'Jem, Miller, listen to me. I'm not asking you to go all soft. I'm telling you there's a way of doing things that is smarter than Diablo and his sort. Don't you see? We make a big show of it, make a fuss, and let the *Mermaid* be known in all the ports as the ship that takes no slaves. A few months of doing things my way, the word gets around. So the *Mermaid* draws alongside another trader. He knows he's doomed. What does he do? Does he fight to the death, killing as many of us as he can before we damage his hull so badly he goes to the bottom and we go hungry? No! A sensible man thinks, "I'll lose my ship but save my skin", and runs down his flag without a shot being fired.'

'Nonsense,' muttered Brasher. 'Never heard of such a thing.'

'Hmmm,' Jem was murmuring. 'It could work.'

'Aye, it makes some sort of sense,' said Miller, reluctantly, 'but what if the captain's never heard of us?'

'Then he'll fight, and we'll give him as good a fight as he deserves,' I said. 'But there's more than one way to climb a mast, eh?'

'Well,' said Jem, getting slowly to his feet. 'There's plenty to be thinking on. Let's get these sails stowed. I've a feeling the weather's about to break, and we'd best be prepared. We'll talk more tomorrow before we dock.'

'If we be real old-style pirates, we'll have pudding every night,' Moggia sang out as he went below.

'And Madeira!' called Ricardo.

Carlo and I cleared away the plates and empty mugs. He was smiling to himself, and when I caught his eye, he winked and turned to clamber down below. I stayed on deck in the rising breeze, watching the clouds flit past the stars and darken the sky.

Jem finished furling the smaller sails and came to

stand beside me, leaning with one hip against the rails. 'You haven't got Cookie to care for you now,' he said. 'You'd best sleep in the cabin if there's rain coming. Anyway, you'll need the chart table.' He grinned. 'You're a navigator now, girl.'

My own cabin? I felt my body fill with amazement. I'd never had a room to myself before, not at home, not ever, and the hole under Cookie's galley bench didn't count. Nobody had a cabin on this ship. Even on *Gisella*, only Diablo had his own room, that spacious salon with ornately carved Spanish furniture. All the other cabins were crammed full of junk, and the men slept in hammocks slung close together in the stinky air below deck.

But on the *Mermaid* there was only one cabin, built for the captain, in the stern of the ship. It was a tiny, dark nook, with one chair, a washbasin, a wooden trunk, and barely enough room to hang a hammock. A door with a brass latch. A hook for wet-weather gear and another for the captain's sword-belt. One wall was taken up by the chart table, the medicine chest, and a fine cabinet for the navigation equipment. Now it was mine.

I'd cleaned up the cabin only the day before. The table had been cluttered with papers and maps — Diablo had taken many of the charts, but not all. In a dark wooden box lay a quadrant, gleaming brass. It was just like my father's, which Lucas and I had taken on our sailing jaunts and tramps all over the island. With a set of navy charts and that quadrant, we could have navigated all over the Mediterranean and right around the world, we'd boasted to each other. We'd let loose the sheets and drift for hours in the hot sun, our feet up on the gunwales, waiting for a nibble on the fishing line, watching the gulls soar high over our mast.

Lucas. How long until I see your funny crinkly smile again? I gazed to the west, as if wishing could bring me closer to Mama and home.

The night was becoming chill. There was a tremendous clattering and thumping somewhere below — probably Carlo falling down the ladder again. I snuggled my coat around me and got ready to go below, to my cabin.

Before he climbed out on the bowsprit to check the sails, Jem stopped for a quiet word with Brasher, who was still nursing his wounds.

'Matey, would you have time to run us up a Maltese flag, just in case we need to pretend we're someone we aren't? And how about a new pennant afore we strike Valletta? Something red and gold and not too fearsome?'

Brasher grinned toothlessly. 'I'll come up with something, lad, never you fear.'

8.
The way of the sea

The wind blew up fiercely overnight, just as Jem had predicted, and when I climbed on deck before dawn we were running with the gale and away from Valletta. Max, still sore from the wound in his ribs, was struggling with the tiller, so I handed him a mug of coffee and took a turn. It took all my strength just to keep us on course. The larboard rails were dipping deep into green water as we scudded through the tops of the waves. Within minutes I was soaked to the skin, and rain coursed down my neck and back. I couldn't help but laugh out loud.

Max patted me on the shoulder, smiling up at the straining sails. 'Aye, lass, she's a beauty, in't she?'

I didn't have any spare muscles left for nodding, so I just grinned.

Max pointed to a long smudge of grey on the horizon. 'There's the Maltese coast yonder, but we won't be docking anywhere tonight, that's for sure. You've got your wish, Cyg. We'll be leagues from here by nightfall.'

'Not if I can help it,' Jem's voice came from behind us. 'Bring her up into the wind. Ricardo, give Cyg a hand.'

'You on deck!' Jem shouted down. 'Reef the mainsail!'

'Ah, matey, we can't bring her around in this,' Max complained.

'I didn't say we were. Just a couple of points should do it. We don't want to be out in this weather. I've a feeling there's a gale on its way. We'll need to find shelter.'

I'd been studying the charts until late into the night. The coastline appeared as rugged as Santa Lucia, but with watchtowers and forts on the headlands. The Knights of Malta guarded their sea lanes like jealous husbands.

'Can we cut around Gozo and seek out an anchorage?' I asked.

'Good idea.' Jem nodded. 'Let's keep out of the shipping channels until we decide what kind of damn pirates we really are. We'll stay close to Malta, but we'd best not land on the main island just yet. If this wind keeps up, we'll be safe enough in Shipwreck Bay.'

'If this wind keeps up, we could be in some cosy Sicilian tavern for supper,' said Ricardo.

'Or smashed to pieces on some cosy Sicilian cliff,' Jem joked. 'No, I fear we're a little further west than we mean to be, so we'll skirt around the islands and find shelter. It's going to be a rough night.'

The day turned out to be rough enough. I plotted the course for Jem and checked it twice. He kept us reefed and well away from the cliffs as we skirted the islands in search of safe harbour. Past San Dimitri Point, the wind calmed a little, and we came at last to anchor in a bay with a stony beach. Even here, the wind was chopping the water. A few small fishing boats, brightly painted, were pulled up on the rocks. It looked like everyone was expecting a big blow.

Jem sent a boat into shore to trade for some fish and fresh water, but there was no rest for us yet. He had the men stash the sails and tie down anything that might move in a storm.

Carlo and I baked extra loaves in case we had to douse the fires later. He was in high spirits, singing as he worked, and I laughed as he tried to reach a note several octaves too high for his deep voice.

'What is that? You sound like a tomcat.'

'Don't say such a thing. I am singing a hymn to Our Lady. Tomorrow, I think, is the Feast of the Assumption. It is a great day.'

'How is it that your people are so pious, but also pirates?' I asked. 'Forgive me. I mean no offence by that,' I added quickly.

'There is no offence. My family are not pirates as these men are pirates.' He waved a flour-covered hand. 'We are, if you like, crusaders.'

'The Crusades are long gone, Carlo.'

'Not in my country. We crusade against the Infidels. We take their ships, we take them prisoner, and one day we will take back the Holy Land.'

This was the territory of the Knights of Malta, the licensed pirates of the Mediterranean, noblemen from the great families of Europe, who sailed from their mystical city of Valletta in galleys powered by Turkish slaves. They were messengers from God, or so they claimed, and defenders of the Faith. Richer than the Pope, it was said, who called on the Knights of the Cross when there was pirate work to be done on behalf of Rome: burning Ottoman ships or bearing soldiers across the sea.

Two hundred years ago, the Knights had defended their island fortress against the Ottoman fleet, and they guarded it to this day from their luxurious palaces. The richest, most powerful of them all was the Grand Master. I had heard so many tales of the fortress city and its people: every noblewoman wore silk and ermine, every Knight had a silver sword and his own fleet, the harbour glittered with golden pennants, and the cathedral bells could be heard across all three islands of Malta. This was Carlo's world.

'You take the Infidels prisoner, they take you prisoner, Diablo takes everyone prisoner,' I grumbled. 'It makes no sense.'

'It is the way of the sea, Cygno. That is all.'

'Tell me, Carlo, what do you think of your El Capitán de Diablo now?'

'He is not a gentleman.' Carlo shook his head, his dark curls twitching. 'I do not like him.'

'When I first met you —'

'Pah! I was young. Since then I have been in combat. Now I am a man. I understand things.'

I leaned down to nudge the tray closer to the embers, smiling to myself. Carlo was only a couple of years older than me, yet sometimes he seemed as young as Lucas. But he was brave enough.

'I've been in combat, too,' I reminded him.

'That soldier. He would not have fallen to you if

I had not weakened him first in a mighty duel.'

At that I laughed out loud. Carlo looked shocked. 'Cygno! Do not mock me. It is true.'

I don't think I'd laughed like that the whole time I'd been away from home. I laughed until tears ran down my face, and the more I laughed, the more Carlo protested, and the funnier he seemed.

'You did not see me, Cygno. I fought like a demon! Slashing here, thrusting there. I nearly had him at the point of my sword. Why do you laugh? It was not funny. I could have been slaughtered. But no. I fought back.'

'Carlo, I'm sorry. I don't mean to laugh.'

I tried to keep from chuckling, but it burst from me again, and I hid my face in my hands.

'It is undignified, to laugh so.' Carlo was quiet now.

'It is. I'm sorry.' I knew I had hurt his feelings.

He was silent for a long moment.

'If you meet my father,' he said, at last, 'you will not tell him that you and I fought the same man, and that you . . . won.'

I peered at his face through the smoke and steam of the tiny galley. He was crouched by the fire, staring into the flames.

'Carlo, you are my friend,' I said. 'I may joke with you here, aboard our ship, but I would never bring you dishonour.'

'You will not tell him I worked in the kitchen like a slave?'

'I will never even lay eyes on your father, not in a hundred years, Carlo. He is a duke. I'm a fisherman's daughter. You mustn't worry.'

'Promise me this.' His gaze was on my face now, intent and pleading.

'Of course, I promise.'

He smiled, relaxed. 'I will soon be home.'

'You're lucky. Your father will be happy.'

I couldn't hide my jealousy. It tasted like vinegar in my mouth.

If you come from wealth, your freedom can be bought like a barrel of salt fish. If you're poor, like me, you have to content yourself with dreams of home, with fantasies of making your own fortune.

I knew now that the crew wouldn't let me go. They weren't as vicious as many men on the high seas — some of them I even liked, and some of them liked me. But while they had a use for me, they wouldn't set me free. I was a slave as surely as those men shackled in *Gisella*'s miserable hold.

All I could do now was to make my own way, take whatever chances were blown into my path. It might take months or years. But one day, just like Carlo, I would return home with honour.

Even if I had to become a pirate myself.

9.
An unexpected guest

Miller's voice echoed through the ship. 'All hands on deck!'

The men scrambled to get out of their hammocks to start the day. It had been a rotten night of lashing gales and a nasty swell, even in our protected inlet, and we'd had little sleep. I made my way to the galley and was struggling to get the fire started, cursing the damp kindling and useless flint, when Miller called out for me.

'You're wanted on deck!'

'Send Carlo down with some more wood,' I hollered. 'I'll be there in a moment.'

'Now!' Miller shouted. 'We've got company.'

'Hell's bum,' I muttered. 'What's the rush?'

There was no spark at all, so I gave up, threw the flint down, stuck the dagger in my belt and went to see what all the noise was about. The sky above was still dense with grey cloud, but there was a strange yellow glare. I didn't like the look of it.

As my hands reached the top rung, I could sense something was wrong. I poked my head out of the hatch.

'Good morning, Lily.'

The voice came from somewhere behind me.

I spun around on the ladder. Hussein Reis, in his blue robes, stood with one hand on Jem's shoulder and one fist around the grip of his scimitar.

'Please join us.'

He motioned to me with his sword. I clambered up and onto the deck.

He was not alone. His crew stood in a circle around Jem and the boys. There were no weapons drawn, besides the scimitar in Hussein's hand, but the air was bright with anger and distrust. You could almost see it.

I took a few steps towards Hussein. His eyes were so blue they seemed almost clear, like the water in a rock pool.

'We have met before, I'm sure you recall.'

I nodded. My hand was on my dagger.

'Then perhaps you'd care to explain what you are all doing here. Without Diablo. On this very pretty little ship. None of the men feel the need to tell me.'

Jem's face had no expression. I couldn't tell what he wanted me to do. Miller was staring at the water. Only Carlo seemed to be watching us, and he was no use. There was nothing for it but to follow my instincts.

'It's a prize, sir. Diablo took her, a week or so ago, and sent us on to Valletta to sell her off.'

'A prize?' Hussein raised one eyebrow.

'Yes, sir.'

'But it seems such a small reward.' He gazed around him at the *Mermaid* and up into her rigging. 'It seems strange that Diablo would chase a prize when, as you at least are aware, Lily, he had other plans.'

'Just greedy, I expect, sir. There was another ship, too, but we sank her.'

'I see.'

He released his grip on Jem's shoulder and stepped towards me.

'Where is Diablo now?'

I tried to peek over his shoulder at Jem for guidance. He was glaring at the back of Hussein's head.

Perhaps Diablo had double-crossed Hussein. One word from me might set the *taridha* after him, chasing him across the Mediterranean and away from Santa Lucia forever.

'He's headed for Algiers.'

'What?' Hussein grabbed my shoulder, his fingers digging into my arms.

'He said he had business there that couldn't wait.'

'What sort of business?'

'I don't know, sir. He didn't say.'

Hussein whirled around.

'You there! Master McGuire. What did he tell you?'

'Nothing, sir,' Jem said sullenly. 'Diablo don't tell me his plans, nor any of us.'

Hussein strode to the starboard rails and stared thoughtfully at his own ship. 'Bring the girl to my cabin.'

Jem stepped forward. 'Sir, she's done nothing wrong.'

But Hussein was already leaping across to his ship.

'I wouldn't argue, if I were you, Master McGuire. Your captain ordered you into Valletta, and yet I find you here, leagues away, clearly with no intention of carrying out his orders. I should have you flogged.'

'We're just riding out the storm, sir,' said Miller.

'Explain that to Diablo!' Hussein bellowed. 'Now bring me the girl.'

Rough hands grabbed me and bundled me over the side. I was half-dragged, half-pushed across the *taridha* and into a cabin lit by candles and oil lamps. All over the floor were rich red carpets, and in the corner, waiting impatiently, stood Hussein Reis. He had flung his sword onto the bed. That, at least, made me feel a little easier. I still had my dagger. If it came to a fight, I would attack like a fury.

But he hardly seemed to know I was there. He paced back and forth from the window to the low bed. His hands were behind his back, his fingers tapping together. His bare feet sounded like drum beats on the carpets. At last he turned to me.

'Tell me everything you saw, Lily. It's important.'

Why should I tell you anything? I thought, sullen as Jem had been on deck. As always, Hussein seemed to know my thoughts.

'I know you don't want to talk to me,' he sighed. 'Why should you? But let's pretend I am the lesser of two fairly vile evils.'

I snorted, and he smiled faintly.

'So.' He looked at me expectantly. 'Let's talk about what I know and what you know. We both know that Diablo had decided to sail to Isola di Bravo, and you had agreed, obviously under duress, to take him into the Golden Grotto. What I need to know is why he changed his mind. Do you have any idea, Lily?'

I shook my head. It had been so long since anyone had called me by my real name, it seemed strange, and somehow comforting, to hear the word. Lily. I wanted him to say it again.

'Think about it. Did he change his mind before he decided to chase the *Mermaid*, or afterwards?'

I did think about it. It was a very interesting question. What on earth was Diablo doing?

'It was afterwards, I think,' I said, tentatively. 'He set course for Isola di Bravo, sure enough. Then they sighted the sails and he took off after them.'

Hussein waited, silently. I thought it through some more.

'He sent off more men than he needed in the prize crew, kept only the Egyptians and the Frenchmen,' I said. 'We thought he had sailed west to meet you and raid the Spanish shipping lanes.'

'No, there was no such plan.'

'I don't know then. I'm sorry.'

'Please, sit,' he said, 'I have been inhospitable. My apologies. I'm as bad as Diablo, perish the thought.'

He waved me to a cushion beside a low table.

'You must have coffee. I imagine you've never tasted coffee such as we serve.'

He called to someone outside, in a language I didn't know. A boy brought tiny cups of thick brown coffee and a dish of sweetmeats.

'Please, help yourself.'

On the table was a bowl of emerald glass, filled with dates and pomegranates.

'I was thinking . . . ' I began. 'Well, we've been trying to work out where he's gone. Diablo, I mean. None of us know, I can promise you that. Not Jem, not anybody.'

'I take your word for it, Lily.'

'So there must have been something about the ships, or something on the ships, that made him change course.'

'Such as?'

I took a sip of the coffee. It was like syrup.

'French soldiers.'

Hussein sat up. 'Armed?'

'Yes,' I nodded. 'We fought them. Diablo took the rest with him as prisoners.'

'Officers?'

'All dead. The captain shot himself, and Diablo killed the others with his bare hands.'

He grasped my arm to draw me closer. 'Did he take their papers?'

I struggled free of his grip.

'I don't know. I suppose so.'

There was silence for a moment.

'Did you see their charts?'

'Why, yes. We still have them. I've been studying them for days.'

'Good. There may be some clue there.'

'I don't know. They are nothing unusual.'

He jumped to his feet and started pacing again.

'Sir?'

'What is it, child?'

'We did wonder what the Frenchmen were doing on an Alexandrian convoy.'

'Indeed,' said Hussein. 'I wonder the same thing.'

'Either it hadn't really sailed from Egypt at all, or . . . '

'Yes?'

'They were on the way back to Egypt, or somewhere thereabouts. Maybe they saw us before we saw them. They might have changed course to trick us.'

He stopped his pacing, and slapped his hands against his legs. 'Well, there's nothing to be done now.'

His tone was lighter. I breathed a little easier.

'Please, Lily. Take a pomegranate.'

'Thank you, sir. I've never really had one.'

'Have you not? How strange.'

'I've seen them, though,' I added, in case he thought I was stupid. I held the pomegranate tight in both hands.

He smiled at me.

'So tell me, did you fight the Frenchmen yourself, with that little dagger?'

'Oh, no, sir,' I said, laughing, 'of course not.'

'I thought not.'

'It was a short-sword,' I said.

His smile vanished, and his eyes widened. 'I beg your pardon?'

'I didn't mean to be in the fighting, sir. It just happened.'

'Good God, girl, what do you mean? You fought a grown man? With a sword?'

'Don't worry, I won.'

It was my turn to smile, as he stared at me, astonished, then threw his head back and let out a loud peal of laughter.

'Ah dear,' he said eventually, 'I think old Diablo is safer wherever on earth he's gone.'

He clapped his hands, and the boy reappeared in the doorway. 'Call Jem McGuire.'

A few minutes later, after I'd scoffed the last of the sweets, Jem shuffled in, reluctantly.

'There you are, Master McGuire. Please sit down.'

'I'll stand, if you don't mind,' said Jem.

'As you please,' said Hussein. 'Let us get straight to the business at hand. You and your crew, I believe, are headed for Valletta?'

Jem nodded.

'I have a small commission I need you to undertake before you do so. Needless to say, I will pay you.'

'I don't know, sir. Diablo sent us —'

'I don't think he'd mind you doing me this little favour, as in fact he had agreed to do it himself, after your trip to Isola di Bravo. He is clearly unable to undertake the work himself, so you will have to step into his boots. You are still his crew, I take it?'

'Yes, of course,' said Jem, blushing.

'I thought as much.'

I wondered just how clearly Hussein could guess what we'd been planning. Did he know everything?

'It's nothing much,' Hussein continued. 'Simply something to be collected. We will speak of it later, in more detail. In the meantime, bring me the charts you found on the *Mermaid*. I will return them to you this afternoon, before I leave.'

'But where are you going?' I spoke without thinking, but he didn't seem to mind.

'I am sailing in search of your wayward captain.'

10.
A game of bluff and chance

That evening, Jem returned from another meeting aboard the *taridha* with the bundle of charts and our orders from Hussein Reis. He called us together.

'Mates, it looks like we won't be docking in Valletta tonight, after all.'

Miller was watching his friend's face, a smile playing on his lips.

'First we return Carlo to the Old City,' said Jem, 'and then we've planned a raid — nothing too flash — but Hussein says we've got to keep it quiet.'

'Never thought I'd see the day when we'd take orders from a Turk,' muttered Brasher.

'What's this raid for, anyhow?' asked Miller.

Jem shook his head. 'I don't rightly know yet. I've got a letter, explaining it all, to be opened when we're close in.'

'Let's see it,' said Miller.

'Lot of good it'd do you, Milly.'

'You can't read neither, Jem — don't know why you're sounding so smug.'

Carlo pushed his way to the front. 'I shall read the letter!'

Jem tucked the paper inside his shirt. 'That wouldn't do, son. You'll be home soon enough, and we can't have you telling your people any private pirate business.'

'I would never tell,' Carlo said, defiantly.

'Never mind that, now. You'll be safe at home by the time we get to open the letter.'

Jem's voice took on a new, decisive tone. 'After we anchor, we'll have to work inland a fair way towards the boy's home, so we'll just take a small party. You two —' Francesco and Ricardo exchanged a wink at this '— and Milly. Me and Cyg.'

Miller looked shocked. 'Hey, why do we have to take the kid?'

I almost agreed with him.

'Hussein has some crazy idea that she can talk her way out of a sticky spot,' Jem said. 'Can't argue with that. You never know, Milly, she might come in handy. For a start, she can read that damn letter to us.'

Miller groaned and Jem punched his shoulder. 'Don't fret, mate. If we're lucky, she'll get lost in the dark.'

'Hey!' I protested. They all sniggered.

'Listen up,' Jem went on. 'We'll have to head back the way we came to avoid the watchtowers, and around towards Moonlight Cove. No need to plot a course, Cyg — the Vella brothers know the coast well enough. Max and Moggia will stand watch on deck while we're ashore. We'll take the boy and collect the ransom fee. Hussein is sending word to the family overland. Then we have another visit to pay and we're away.'

I tried to avoid Carlo's gaze. I would be sorry to see him go, and I knew that for all his talk he would miss being part of this crew.

'That's all,' said Jem. 'Weigh anchor!'

The others scrambled to haul the anchor up off the sand. Jem stopped me as I ran to join the men hauling on the halyards to make some sail.

'There's another thing. I'm to look after you, Hussein says.'

'I don't need looking after, Jem.'

At this he grinned. 'Aye, that's what he says. But I'm to do it anyway.'

'What's it to him?' I stared up at Jem's face, but there was no hint of what might have passed between the two men.

Jem shrugged. 'No understanding some people, eh? He must think you're precious or something.'

I blinked, trying to reconcile this with the Hussein Reis of legend, the killer of innocents, with his mighty scimitar and pitiless crew.

'I tried to tell him you were only shark bait,' Jem joked, 'but he wouldn't listen. Now, off you go — the boys'll need a hand with the headsail.'

From up in the bow I peered over at the *taridha* as we moved out of the bay. Hussein Reis was nowhere to be seen. No doubt he was still pacing in his carpeted cabin or poring over charts, trying to guess where Diablo had gone. Good luck to you, I thought. Who in their right mind would go looking for Diablo?

It took the best part of a day to beat back along the coast against a stiff breeze, far enough out from the shore to avoid any watching eyes. Jem was sailing for a deserted bay where we could anchor unseen while the shore party carried out its plans.

'The Knights have watchtowers all around the islands. It's best if they don't know we're here,' he told me. 'We have one of Malta's favourite sons on board as a hostage, and no doubt they'd be happy to take him back by force rather than ransom. So we'll keep out of sight, do what we came here to do. We'll fly the flag of the Maltese Cross as an extra precaution. Then in a few days we can sail into Valletta and act innocent as lambs.'

If only it had been that simple.

We rowed into Moonlight Cove in the ship's launch just before midnight. Max had orders to leave the bay if he sighted any strange vessels; otherwise he'd wait there for two days and two nights. If we didn't return, he was to sail around the island to the harbour city in the hope of meeting us there.

All the men were nervous — once the *Mermaid* sailed into Valletta's Grand Harbour, it would be the end of our brief spell of freedom. The ship would be seized and sold off like any pirate prize, while the men would rot in harbour waiting for Diablo to return. Carlo would be home with his father, and I would find some way of getting home too. Not that the crew knew it, of course, although Jem must have had his suspicions.

So we all had a great deal riding on our secret mission for Hussein Reis.

The boat was unsteady, ploughing through the choppy water. I braced myself with one knee hard against the ribs of the boat. Behind me, an odd squeal was followed by an enormous splash.

'Jesus wept,' Jem groaned. 'He's fallen overboard again. Belay rowing!'

I spun around in my seat just in time to see two wet hands groping for the gunwales.

'Drag him in, lads, and easy does it or we'll all end up in the drink,' said Jem.

The Vella brothers leaned over the side and chanted like schoolboys, 'One, two, three!' On the last count, they hauled Carlo, gasping and splashing like the morning catch, back into the boat.

We hit the pebbly shore, and climbed out of the boat slowly and a little shakily. My legs were unsteady after all those weeks at sea. Carlo waved goodbye to the boat crew and stood watching them row back to the *Mermaid* until Miller gave him a shove.

'C'mon, lad. We're expected at your father's house.' He kept up a flood of questions as the Vella brothers led the way up the cliff, along a narrow ledge, and across the grasslands.

'Does your father have a night watch?'

'There is usually a man on the door, but he is not armed,' Carlo said.

'And the rest of your family, will they be at home?'

'I don't know.' Carlo seemed more solemn with every stumbling step he took. 'There's only my mother. My brother is grown up — he has his own *palazzo* in the countryside.'

'I hope they're expecting us, or there'll be hell to pay,' said Miller. 'Jem, how long would Hussein's messenger have taken?'

'Don't worry. It's all been arranged. We take the boy to the house, collect the gold, and that's it. Back to the ship. Good night's sleep. Sail away on the morning breeze and get on with the rest of it.'

'It's too simple,' said Miller. 'Nothing can be that easy.'

He's right, I thought. Nothing is ever that easy. I joined Miller in his questioning.

'Carlo, your house, is it fenced?'

'There is a walled courtyard at the rear.'

'But the front of the house?'

'Just the door leading into the hallway.'

'Aha!' said Miller. 'A good place for a trap.'

'How high is the rear wall?' I asked.

Carlo was getting impatient. 'My father is a man of honour. If he has agreed to pay, he will pay.'

'See?' said Jem. 'All will be well.'

I had an uneasy sense of foreboding deep in my belly. Miller dropped back to walk along beside me.

'Are you having the same fears as me?' he asked.

I nodded. 'You're right. It's too simple. Why would any noble house pay such a huge amount to a pack of ruffians when they could have the boy and keep the gold? All they need to do is have a quiet word to the city sentries and we'd be trapped like crayfish.'

'Aye.'

'Carlo,' I called out, 'have you ever climbed the courtyard wall?'

'Of course, many times. It is the only way of

escaping my tutor and his boring Latin.'

Ricardo held up his hand for quiet. 'Keep your voices down now. We skirt around a village, and the dogs will hear you yapping at each other.'

'How much further?' I asked. I was tired already from the long walk, slogging up dusty hills and sliding down gravel gullies. Before we'd set off, I'd grabbed a long coil of rope from the deck and looped it over my shoulders. You never know when you'll need a good length of rope. But about half an hour after we'd started walking, I was regretting bringing the damn thing. Still, there was no way I would ask anyone to carry it or dump it by the track, so I trudged on.

'Another hour to the city walls, then we must find the way in.'

Carlo's family lived in the ancient capital, the Old City, perched high on a hill above the centre of the island. With the moon behind us, we crouched in a hollow and peered up towards the great arched gateway and the massive walls. There were only two gates into the city, and both were guarded. The Old City was silent, but up on the bastions the guards were standing rigid on their watch.

I peered about. 'Where's Francesco?' I whispered.

'He knows a way through the walls — a smuggler's door,' Ricardo said quietly, 'but it has been so long, we must be sure it is still safe. He has gone to see.'

Someone hissed from lower down the path. Jem cocked his pistol, and I put my hand on my dagger.

Ricardo let out a low whistle, which was answered. Within minutes, Francesco was with us, panting from his run through the dark along the fortifications.

'I cannot find it,' he whispered. 'I have failed.'

'Saints and angels above,' Miller muttered.

'I am sorry. There is no way into the city except through the gates. The smuggler's door has been bricked up, I think. I cannot see it anywhere.'

'Neptune's teeth!' Jem swore. 'Now what do we do?'

'What was meant to happen?' I asked.

Jem looked more cross than I'd ever seen him. 'There was supposed to be . . . ' he spat in Francesco's direction, 'a secret door in through the convent.'

Miller spluttered. 'Pirates in a convent? I wish I'd a-seen that.'

'It is a sight you will never see, for now all is lost,' sighed Ricardo. 'They are very beautiful, too, some of those younger sisters.'

'How can you say such things?' Carlo asked. 'It is blasphemy.'

'I have seen them!' Ricardo retorted.

'The Convent of St Benedict? They never admit any men, especially such sinners as you.'

If they carried on like this, I might have to bang their heads together.

'Shut up, you two,' I hissed. 'Any more noise and you'll have the whole guardhouse out here searching for us.'

I glanced up at Jem, who was still crouched, staring at the ramparts. 'What do we do now?' I asked.

'How am I supposed to know? I never been here afore!'

At that, I lost all patience and stood up. 'This is ridiculous.'

I grabbed Carlo's sleeve and pulled him to his feet. 'You come with me. Jem, you too.'

'Sit down, Cyg!' Jem whispered hoarsely. 'You're not going anywhere.'

'None of us are, at this rate. We have to do something. Come on, Carlo. The rest of you stay here, and if you hear any commotion, run for it or start shooting to draw their attention or something like that. Miller, you'll know what to do.'

He nodded. 'I'll think of something.'

'Are you coming or not, Jem?'

I started scrambling towards the gate, holding Carlo's hand tight in mine. Behind us, Jem was running to catch up.

'Cygno,' Carlo whispered, 'do you have a plan?'

'Not really,' I admitted. 'After all, we don't have too many choices. The only thing to do is to walk up to the gate and ask to be let in.'

'Are you mad?' Jem was now striding alongside us.

'Perhaps,' I said. Maybe I was mad, but a very long walk in the middle of the night with a pack of bumbling pirates was enough to drive anybody crazy.

As our feet hit the smooth flagstones of the bridge, Jem grabbed my arm. 'Quick, get back before they see us.'

But it was too late. The guard's challenge rang out loud and clear. 'Halt! You cannot pass. The gates are closed until dawn.'

We stopped still in the middle of the bridge.

'Tell him who you are, Carlo,' I said softly.

'What?' Jem spluttered. 'Don't you dare.'

Carlo's eyes flicked from my face to Jem's. In the moonlight, so close to home, he was torn between two loyalties and a mounting fear.

The guard cried out again. 'Who goes there?' There was a rattle of keys and the gliding thunk of a heavy bolt, as a manhole in the huge wooden gate swung open.

'Tell them you've been kidnapped by pirates and have finally found your way here,' I instructed Carlo, working it out as I spoke. 'They will escort you home.'

'But you, Cygno?' he asked.

'I'll come with you.'

'No!' Jem retorted. 'I'm not losing both hostages in one night.'

I patted his chest. 'You aren't losing any hostages, Jem. You're coming too. Just play your cards carefully and everything will be fine.'

The guards' boots were thudding on the bridge.

'It's too late to argue, Jem,' I pleaded. 'Trust me.'

Carlo took a huge breath, filling his lungs with air and courage, and turned to face the patrol. 'At last,' he cried, throwing his arms open wide. 'My countrymen!'

The sentries halted, confused, just in front of the gate. One of them, a sergeant of the city watch, stepped forward, eyeing us suspiciously. 'Who goes there?'

'It is I, Carlo St Angelo de Santiago. I am returned!'

11.
The Old City

The soldiers clustered before the city gates and looked at each other as if the bedraggled young man before them was crazed from too much wine. Carlo took one step forward.

'You know my father, of course? My great-uncle was a Knight Grand Cross.'

The sergeant appeared sceptical. 'Who'd you say you were again?'

'I am Carlo, son of the Duke de Santiago. If you would kindly escort us home, my father will remember your kindness, I am sure.' At this, he bowed deeply. 'Let us proceed.'

At a signal from the sergeant, the guards raised their muskets.

'You can come, but not those two.'

Carlo glanced around at us. I held my breath and stared at him steadily and meaningfully. This was his chance to escape and save his father the ransom money. Jem and the others could do nothing now. I wouldn't have blamed Carlo for running for the gate. One shout of 'Pirates, help me!' and the patrol would protect him and shoot us down where we stood. Jem was standing firm, so I did too. I didn't know whether it was scarier to go forward or run and take my chances of getting a musket ball in the back.

'These are my servants,' Carlo said in an even, almost relieved tone. 'They have protected me through many dangers. They must accompany me to my father's house.'

I let go in a rush the breath I'd been holding, and heard Jem swear quietly beside me.

'All right then, I'll escort you myself,' the sergeant announced, 'and no nonsense, or you'll march straight into the dungeons.'

Jem grunted something unintelligible and probably very rude as we trudged forward and finally passed through the grand archway into the Old City. Six guards appeared from nowhere to clatter along behind us, swords drawn, as we entered the ancient city. Carlo strode ahead, chatting to the sergeant as if he'd known him all his life.

'The dungeons!' he called out to us, pointing to a grim-looking staircase descending into darkness just inside the gate. He flashed a wicked smile.

'This all part of the plan, I suppose?' said Jem, scarcely bothering to hide the sarcasm in his voice.

But I couldn't speak. Before us was the city, quiet in the moonlight. Massive, wondrous buildings lined the streets, pale limestone, with balconies of woven iron and carved wood. I had never seen such palaces. I'd never seen so many big buildings all at once — they formed a tunnel through which we marched, Jem shuffling behind the guards with his hand firmly around his dagger. At each corner, he peered down the twisting alleys as if expecting an ambush. At least someone was paying attention — I was too awestruck to worry about what might happen next.

Our steps echoed off the smooth walls, and each *palazzo* we passed revealed a beauty and life of its own. At a window, behind half-open shutters, a lamp had been lit, and a golden pool of light spilled out onto the road. From another house, a delicate white curtain billowed in the breeze like a fairy ship's sail. There was music, someone playing a cello very softly, and a woman's voice calling goodnight to an unseen child.

We passed the *piazza*, and there, towering over all the houses, stood the greatest building I'd ever seen. I must have gasped, for Carlo turned and grinned.

'The cathedral,' he explained. 'San Paulo.'

'It's beautiful,' I whispered, almost to myself.

'Hurry along,' grumbled the sergeant, 'this isn't a bleedin' Grand Tour.'

'Have you ever seen such glory?' Carlo cried, skipping across the cobblestones.

'This way!' He led us down an alleyway which twisted left, then right, and stopped before the enormous carved doors of a house that towered above our heads. 'Now, Cygno, welcome to my home.'

He banged hard on the door with its mighty bronze knocker, calling out in a language I did not understand. The door opened a crack, and we heard a gasp.

'*Señor* Carlo!'

A dishevelled old man was standing in the doorway, his arms open. Carlo ran to him, and in an instant they were both laughing and kissing each other's cheeks.

The old man wiped a tear from his eye.

As we stood watching, I felt an awful ache, of emptiness, of loneliness. Carlo was reunited with his family, and I . . . well, I still had to get out of here alive. I took a step forward.

'Carlo, you must introduce us to your father.'

He stared at me a moment, before bursting into laughter.

'No, no, no,' he said, 'this is not my father. This is Alfredo, our manservant.'

At last the soldiers dropped their weapons. 'If you don't mind, young sir, we'll be getting along now.'

'Of course.' Carlo waved them away. 'Thank you for your services. We will send some reward to the guardhouse tomorrow.'

'As you will, sir,' said the sergeant with a nod. 'If you're sure these ruffians are welcome in your house?'

'Indeed. They are like family to me.' Carlo was laying on all the charm he could muster.

The sergeant barked at his men, and they clattered along the narrow street and back towards the gate. I relaxed a little. One problem out of the way.

'Come, come,' cried Carlo, taking my arm and dragging me into the hallway. 'We must go find my father at once. Alfredo says he's in his library.'

Inside the house, the walls were smoothed stone and hung with cloth, rich and glorious. Our bare feet seemed even dirtier than usual on the tiled floor. I looked up. Painted scenes of ships in battle and the clash of great armies swirled around the ceiling. Mounted above the door were broadswords, the weapons of the crusaders, and a shield, red with a white cross.

'No time for gawking, Cyg,' said Jem, roughly, as he paced down the hallway behind Carlo and the old man, who led the way with a tall candle. Jem turned around to whisper to me.

'I don't know what we do now, but you just keep your hatch shut and leave the figuring to me for once.'

'Yes, Jem,' I nodded, obediently.

Alfredo knocked gently on a door and opened it slowly. There was a harsh voice from inside the room. 'What is it now?'

I stole a glance at Carlo. He was straightening his dirty clothes and smoothing down his rumpled hair. He took a deep breath and stepped into the candle-lit room. Jem and I squeezed through the door behind him.

I gasped. So did Carlo.

His father was standing by an enormous fireplace, staring straight at us. With him was Hussein Reis, one hand on the scimitar in his belt.

There was not a word from Jem, but I could feel his body stiffen in readiness to attack. I quickly studied the layout of the room: two high windows behind the desk, an open door into the next room. There was no one else here.

We all stood in silence. Alfredo bowed out quietly and closed the door behind him.

Hussein, as always, was the first to speak. 'My friends, I didn't expect you here so soon. You've made good time.'

Carlo took a few steps forward. 'Papa?'

'My son!' spat the Duke. There was no pleasure in his face. 'What do you mean, coming here in the dark, like a criminal, with these . . . ?'

'But, Papa —'

'Enough! Get upstairs. Go to your mother. She has been crying for you these last weeks and I can't bear the noise a moment longer.'

Carlo's head sagged down on his chest, as if all the air had gone from his lungs.

'Go now, boy!'

When Carlo turned to face us, there were tears in his eyes.

'Farewell, Carlo,' I said gently. 'The bravest swordsman of the high seas.'

He nodded, and tried to smile, but it didn't work.

The door clicked softly behind him, like a sprung trap. Jem and I exchanged glances, he winked ever so slightly, and we turned towards the two men by the fire.

'You said you were sending word to the family,' Jem said to Hussein. 'Very kind of you to bring the news yourself.'

'Pure coincidence, I assure you,' Hussein said, airily. As he spoke, he walked towards us, slowly and purposefully, until his back was to the Duke. 'I had other business here in the Old City, and thought to pay my respects. A great deal of money is owed to El Capitán de Diablo for the safe return of the boy. I am simply protecting his interests. As you know, he and I are old friends.'

'Pity you didn't just deliver the boy yourself and save us the walk.'

Jem and Hussein were staring into each other's eyes, as if some silent battle was raging between them. I couldn't tell what it was, but it felt dangerous. The Duke was watching them, transfixed.

'Now that we're here,' I piped up, stepping across nearer the Duke, 'I'm very pleased to meet you, sir. Carlo talks about you all the time.'

All three of them switched their gaze to me, and the spell was broken.

The Duke snorted. 'The boy's a fool, and a damned expensive one at that.'

'Speaking of which,' I said, 'if you don't mind too much, we'll be taking the ransom and be on our way. I'm sorry we've interrupted your pleasant evening.'

'Quite.'

He moved to the desk and began shuffling some papers. I watched his hands. He had fine, pale fingers, delicate and long, and trembling. His greying hair was falling down across his forehead, in ringlets like his son's, but beneath his curls his eyes flickered, like blue flames, searching across the room, calculating and dangerous. For all his finery, he seemed like a greyhound, cornered and snarling. I watched as one hand moved towards the desk drawer.

'I trust you're not thinking of doing anything extraordinarily heroic, sir,' I said. 'We have men waiting outside ready to come to our aid.'

'I'm not a fool, child.'

'Nor am I, sir. You're a man of honour, who understands the way of the sea. Carlo has told me that. I do not believe you would renege on a hostage ransom. Please make it ready, in gold, and we'll take our leave.'

At this he simply grunted. 'Gold?' He sneered at Hussein. 'Did you hear the wretched child? Now she wants gold!'

Hussein spread his hands, as if in sympathy, deploring the manners of modern pirates.

'She's smart enough,' he told the Duke. 'The world grows more uncertain every day. She's right to place her trust in gold, not men.'

'Pah!'

I watched them both closely. They bantered like old friends or business rivals. Something was happening beyond my ken — Jem and I were out of our depth, and the sooner we got clear of these two, the better.

A slight twitch of the Duke's left hand caught my eye.

'Look out!'

He moved fast, like a snake, pulling a pistol from the folds of his gown and cocking it to aim at Jem. But Hussein was faster. In a heartbeat he had the Duke's arms pinned behind him. The pistol clattered to the floor and exploded in a fiery crash.

It seemed a thousand angel bells tinkled above us as the vast chandelier shattered in a cloud of crystal shards that floated and crackled across the room. I felt the tiny blades falling all over me, cutting and stabbing like a hundred needles.

'Damn you to hell,' Jem snarled. His face was bloody. All of us were marked with fine red lines, dozens of small cuts on our faces and hands. I could feel them down my back.

The Duke was struggling to get free.

'Run, you idiots,' Hussein shouted.

Jem grabbed my arm.

'The window . . . ' I gasped, 'quickly, over the back wall.'

Jem took the lead, dragged me across the room and kicked open a window with one foot. As we ran over the carpet, more splinters of crystal embedded themselves in the tough soles of our bare feet. It felt like running over rose bushes.

The courtyard was deserted — a dark square of orange trees and paving. As we ran, I sneaked a glance back into the library. Hussein had let go of the Duke, who was slumped in a chair by the fireplace, head in hands. Hussein stood just inside the window, staring out into the night after us.

'Here!' Jem scrambled up a tree and pulled himself up on top of the stone wall. He reached down to help me, both our hands slippery with blood. We dropped gently over the other side into an alley. Far off, we could hear sounds of alarm and clamour, as the city guards sought out the source of the gunshot. They'd be here any minute.

'We'll hide somewhere and wait for daylight.' Jem squinted up at the stars to get his bearings.

'This way!' I started running down the alley.

'Hey!' he called after me. 'Who's in charge here?' I smiled to myself, and kept running. He'd catch up soon enough.

'Where do you think you're going?'

'The city walls,' I panted. 'If there's no way in, there's only one way out.'

'Blackbeard's blood!' he muttered.

We raced down narrow lanes, dodged back across

the main street, passed palaces and old churches and a deserted marketplace. It was hard going. The rope around my shoulder blistered my skin, and I felt trickles of sweat or blood, or maybe both, on my face. The cuts from the chandelier crystal were starting to sting like jellyfish.

At last we came to a quiet corner of the massive wall, built to keep out the invaders of centuries, but not to keep in lost, desperate pirates. Jem peered about, checking for guards or soldiers. There was no one in sight. We worked our way silently along the base of the wall towards a bastion. A flight of steps led up to the ramparts.

We were both panting after our race across the city. 'I hope you know what you're doing,' said Jem. I hoped the same thing. We ran noiselessly up the steps and squeezed behind a pillar to hide from the treacherous moonlight.

'This'll do,' I said, with more confidence than I felt. 'Tie a bowline.'

Jem grabbed the end of the rope from the coil around my shoulders, flung it around the pillar and knotted it quickly. 'If you're going to start acting like a pirate bloody princess you can tie your own damn bowlines.'

'You know I'm not good at knots.'

'Bleedin' hell,' he muttered. 'All right, let's go. I hope whatever's on the other side of that wall is better than what's on this side.'

'Don't worry.' I slapped his shoulder. 'We'll be back on board the *Mermaid* by sunrise.'

'In the dungeon, more like.'

'Out to sea and clear away.'

'Roasted on a spit in the *piazza*.'

'Will you come on?'

'Aye, ma'am.'

He took the rope from me, checked again for the guards in the bastion, and let it fly, uncoiling, through the night air and out over the parapet.

'You first,' said Jem. 'I'll keep a watch. Whistle when you're down.'

'If I can't whistle, I'll scream.'

He chuckled. 'Over you go, then.'

I sneaked a last glance along the empty stone parapets and grabbed the rope in both hands as I clambered onto the edge.

'Keep down,' Jem hissed, and I dropped low. Up here, a cool breeze ruffled the flags and chilled me in an instant. Or maybe it was fear. I crouched between two huge carved blocks of stone. From these ramparts, the soldiers on duty could see clear across the island. In the distance the sea glistened under the moon. I didn't dare look down, but wiped my bloody hands on my shirt and then lowered myself slowly over the edge.

It felt as if the whole of Malta could see me hanging there. I waited for a cry, a shot in the dark. None came.

Hand over hand, I kept going, slowly and surely down the rope, keeping close to the wall. It wasn't so different from racing Carlo down the shrouds, but I was tired, and my muscles began trembling with fear and exhaustion. I tried walking my feet down the rough stone walls — anything to stop me from sliding down too fast. It didn't help. I wrapped my legs tightly around the rope and dug my fingernails deep into it at every grip, until I felt they would rip right out of my fingers. Sweat stung my eyes.

But then, below me, I felt the end of the rope between my bare feet. It was too short. A quick peep down revealed some straggly bushes and dry grassland a long drop away. This, I thought, is what they mean by being caught between a rock and a hard place.

My face toward the sky, I let out a long, low whistle. Jem answered, and a sudden tension on the rope told me he was starting his climb down.

I muttered a silent prayer to St Jude, Hope of the Hopeless, closed my eyes, and let go of the rope.

The fall wasn't as long as I'd expected, but I landed on all fours with a thump and a groan that should have woken the guards all across the island. I lay still, the breath knocked right out of me, unable to breathe, unable to move. But I didn't seem to be dead. Good old St Jude.

High above me came a questioning whistle from Jem, no doubt at the end of the rope and wondering if I'd survived the drop. I summoned the little air in my lungs to answer him, then rolled to one side — the fall hadn't killed me, but if Jem landed on top of me I was a dead duck.

He arrived with an almighty thud and lay where he had landed in the dust. A low moan escaped from his lips.

'Come on, Jem, don't be a girl.'

One of his eyes opened. 'You still alive, then?' he croaked. 'Good. Come here while I murder you.'

I rolled over onto my hands and knees. My wrists and ankles hurt like Hades from the landing, but the rest of me seemed to be working. I spat a little blood out. I'd bitten my bottom lip on impact. Jem lay on his back, wheezing, then slowly lifted each arm and leg, flexing his fingers.

'Still in one piece, then?' I asked.

'Every bone in my body is shattered, but thanks for asking.'

'Not as bad as a musket ball in the back, Jem, you have to admit.'

'I'm not admitting nothing. Wretched child. That's what the Duke called you, but he didn't know the half of it.'

He sat up, gradually and painfully, and glared at me. Uh-oh, I thought, maybe I've pushed him too far this time.

But his eyes crinkled and he threw his head back in a mighty whoop of glee. 'By Drake's beard!' he said out loud. 'I don't know where we are, or how I got landed with you, but that was magnificent.'

I was laughing too now, with relief and amazement.

'Let's go find the boys,' he said, and we linked arms and hobbled into the bushes.

All the way back to the boat we talked through everything that had happened. The others quizzed us, and cheered at Jem's tale of our escape. Although we were covered in bloody cuts, and Jem was limping badly, we were filled with the joy of a close escape and the crisp early-morning air. But so much of our story made no sense. Francesco and Ricardo kept up a rapid-fire of questions — to most there were no clear answers.

'What is Hussein Reis doing in the Old City?'

'There's a price on his head. Is he mad?'

'And why tonight?' asked Miller. 'I don't like the sound of it.'

'Perhaps he will collect our ransom for us?' said Ricardo hopefully.

'Or get thrown in the dungeon for helping us escape,' said Jem.

'Mother Mary!' cried Francesco. 'What will Diablo do to us for giving up the boy for no gold?'

I kept my other thoughts to myself: of poor Carlo's humiliation as he shuffled from the room; of Hussein's blue eyes peering into the dark courtyard after us; of him standing beside a Duke as an equal. There had to be a clue in all of this. I needed time to think.

'Jem?' He was some way behind on the narrow goat-track, leaning on Miller for support as he hobbled along. 'Have you got that letter from Hussein? Those sealed orders he gave you?'

'Aye, right here.' He pulled a crumpled paper from inside his shirt. It was still sealed. I flipped it over.

The letter was addressed to me. Miss Lily Swann.

How did he know my family's name?

'Jem, what did he say when he gave you this?'

He shrugged, trying to remember. 'He asked if any of the rest of us could read, and said to give it to you . . . well, about now, I suppose.'

I tore open the packet with fluttery fingers.

Dear Lily,

It may seem strange that I send you this letter, but I believe that you are capable of both reading it and of following my instructions. The Mermaid is to carry out a mission of some secrecy. Please keep this to yourself until you are off the island after your visit to de Santiago's.

You will find enclosed some bearings for a small cove on the coast near the Cliffs of Dingli. There you will find Ebenezer Black. Mister Black may not feel very friendly towards me, so please don't mention my name. In his possession is a valuable chalice, priceless in fact, from the Grand Master's palace, where Mister Black is a secretary to the Court. It must be in your care when next we meet.

I trust you and the men of the Mermaid to undertake this with a minimum of murder and mayhem. Harm no one. Hurry away and stay close to where we last met. I will find you there.

There was no signature, but underneath a quick sketch of two scimitars, crossed. I read it again, as best I could as the sun peeped over the distant cliffs. Fine, dignified handwriting, orders that brooked no disobedience. Whoever he was, whoever he had been, Hussein Reis was a man to be reckoned with.

Whatever he was playing at, we would have to play along. The *Mermaid* was going into action.

12.
The silver sword

It took less than a day to sail around the island and find the cove with a lonely whitewashed house high on the cliff top. We sailed past in the daylight, pretending not to be gawking, and then doubled back in the dark for our raid later that night. I was down below, listening and waiting, when Miller called down the hatch.

'Jemmy wants you on deck, Cyg. Looks serious, too.'

Lord, I thought, what have I done now?

I scrambled up on deck as fast as my feet would carry me. The crew was gathered in a rough circle around Jem, who stood with a grim face as I approached. There was a sword in his hand.

'What is it, Jem? What's wrong?'

He stared at me for a long moment and finally raised the sword in front of him. My stomach squirmed, and something turned over deep inside me.

Suddenly, he smiled, as wide as I'd ever seen.

'We figured that if you're going to lead a pirate raid, you ought to have a proper weapon.'

He held the sword out to me.

'This is for you, Cygnet, from all of us. Make sure you don't disgrace us.'

They were all beaming at me now.

I gazed up at the blade. I'd never seen anything so beautiful.

'Where did you get this?'

'Let's just say we borrowed it from Diablo.'

I held it in my hands. The hilt was heavy, too large for my small fists, and the guard circled my knuckles with inches to spare. The leather wrapped tight around the grip warmed to my touch. I clenched my fingers and slowly lifted the tip of the blade off the deck and high into the air. The steel glimmered, even in the dark.

'I . . . I've never seen such a sword.'

'It's a scimitar,' said Ricardo. 'Very precious, very famous. The greatest weapon of the Barbary Coast.'

My sword. My very own Excalibur.

'You're a real swashbuckler now, little Cygnet,' Max whispered. 'There's no going back to Santa Lucia.'

He was right, of course, but at that moment I didn't care. I couldn't take my eyes off the inlaid gold tracing fine arabesques along the blade. Long after my shoulder had started aching and I'd had to rest the tip on the deck, I stared at my sword, moved the curved blade ever so slightly to catch the starlight, and wondered at its gleam.

How many men have you killed, friend? I wondered. How many more dark hearts will tremble at your touch?

'Time to go ashore, Cygno,' Moggia whispered.

'Lights are out in the big house.'

I nodded.

'You take the first watch, Max. If we're not back by dawn, up anchor, circle the island, and come back tomorrow after dark.'

'Aye, lass. You'll be back all right.'

I wrapped the scimitar in its oilcloth again and stowed the precious package in the locker below the tiller. It would be small arms only tonight.

I stuck a dagger in my belt and clambered down the ropes into the boat. We made our way quietly into the rocky cove, oars muffled, nobody speaking. The darkness felt like fog against my face. As the boat ground onto the sand, Miller and Francesco leaped out to pull us into shore. With a signal, I sent them all on their way — two small groups of men scrambling over the rocks and up the cliff towards the silent house.

It was a good night for it: cloudy with a light nor'easterly breeze whipping up the grass to mask the sounds of our creeping.

At another hand signal, two men slipped onto the veranda and tried a window or two before they slid one open. Pale curtains fluttered out in the breeze. Two other men crossed the yard to sneak into the barn. They would take whatever they could from the smokehouse, from the granary. Those fat sheep we'd seen through the telescope were safe tonight — no point trying to get beasts back down the cliff — but we might as well eat decent food for a week or two more.

We had other business inside. Jem and I quietly

prised open a back door. The kitchen was cold and stank of old food scraps and cats. Through the archway, we tiptoed through a servants' dining hall and into the main house.

I could hear the chickens kicking up a bit of a fuss in the coop. Gently does it, lads — gently and silently.

We could see a long hallway with many doors and a grand staircase. A gold-framed mirror set our reflections upon us. Jem raised his eyebrows and blew a kiss to himself.

Third door on the left. I tried the door handle. It turned. All too easy so far.

I stepped into the library, Jem close behind me. Ebenezer Black stood in the middle of the room, his musket aimed at my face.

'Hold, scum, or I'll shoot!' he hissed.

'No need to worry, sir,' I whispered. 'We won't harm you. We're only here for the chalice.'

He laughed quietly. 'That's all?'

'No point beating about the harbour, is there, sir? So hand it over and you'll go unharmed.'

His smile was ghastly. Yellow teeth and thin, bitter lips.

'You seem to forget, young lady, that you are the one with the gun aimed at your head.'

'I thank you, sir, for the reminder.' I bowed, ever so slightly. 'But may I remind you that scum such as me rarely travel alone? So you'll no doubt be aware that my men are standing by in your nursery, ready to grab your children should anything go wrong.'

'You're bluffing.'

'I may be. You never know. Let's find out, shall we?' I took a deep breath as if to holler.

'Hold still, I said!' he snapped.

'Hand it over and you'll come to no harm — we'll be gone before you know it.'

'Insolent pup!' His fingers were tightening around the gun. 'Who are you to raid my house in the middle of the night and issue orders like the Grand Master himself?'

'There's your clue, sir.'

'Nonsense. You claim to be a messenger from the Grand Palace? Impossible!'

'He wants no fuss, sir. Allow the chalice to return to its rightful home and you'll hear no more about it.'

'Ha!' Black snorted. 'That proves it. You foolish girl. If the Grand Master wants that damn cup back, all he has to do is ask.'

'Of course,' I nodded knowingly. What on earth was going on here? Nothing for it but to take a chance. 'He gave it to you for safekeeping.'

He shrugged. There was some kind of strange truth in my storytelling. Worth another punt.

'There has been a change of plan, and now the time has come for its return. But he wants it kept quiet.'

Black tried hard to control his demeanour, but a terrible grimace flashed across his face. 'So soon?' he whispered. 'It can't be!'

'You'd best give me the chalice.'

'Never! You expect me to believe this nonsense?'

I sighed.

'Jem,' I motioned at him, 'take the children to the boat.'

'You'll not touch my children!' Black stepped forward, menacingly.

'It's your choice, sir. I'm sure they'll make fine pirate slaves — it's not such a bad thing. I used to be one myself, and you can see how I've turned out.' I grinned in spite of myself, in spite of the danger.

'I'm warning you!'

Enough of this! 'No, I'm warning you, Mister Black. We can slaughter you now and take the chalice or you can save us all the bother. My master will not rest until he has it. Shoot me tonight, and another will come tomorrow. And the night after. You will never sleep safe in your bed again.'

For a long moment, nobody even breathed, but at last he sighed and lowered the gun.

'Take it, the damned thing. I never wanted it anyway. I don't care who sent you. You don't need to make up any more of those silly stories. Leave my children alone.'

He fell backwards, heavily, into a chair, his head sagging down on his chest. Jem scrambled over to the desk and began dragging open the drawers.

'Blast you, where is it, then?' he cried.

I watched Black's eyes flick around the room.

'The bookcase,' I said quietly.

Jem stumbled towards it in the gloom and flung a book on the floor to search behind it.

'Careful with those, Jem, they're precious,' I warned. He looked up at me, shook his head slowly as he did so often, and resumed the search.

The door opened silently, and Miller peered in. 'What's up, Cyg?'

'We'll be ready in a moment,' I replied. 'Gather up the boys. Mister Black's been most obliging, so there's no need to make a fuss.'

'There's a pretty little kitchen maid,' he said hopefully.

'Leave her alone, and get moving.' I tried to sound gruff.

'Aye, Cyg.' He disappeared.

When I turned around, Jem was holding the chalice tight in both hands, mouth agape.

'Come on, wrap it up and get a move on.'

I stepped closer to Black.

'Forgive me, sir, but it might look better if there were signs you'd fought like a tiger.'

He nodded.

'It's only fair — you were game enough,' I said.

A snort, almost a groan.

I waved Jem from the room. 'Get going. Meet me at the boat.'

He ran, and in a moment I heard a low whistle from the yard. At last Black looked up from whatever despair he'd been contemplating.

'Who are you, child?'

'Nobody of consequence.'

'Ha! I assure you it is of some consequence to me. It's not customary, you must admit, for a young girl to be bounding about in the middle of the night with a gang of cut-throats.'

'Tell you a secret, sir, it's the sorriest gang of cut-throats you ever beheld.'

'Now I look at you, you do remind me of someone I knew long ago. What do they call you?'

'Never mind that.'

'Funny, really, that I should be thinking of him now.'

'Your pardon, sir, I must be getting along. You'll excuse me if I just hit you on the head and take my leave.'

'There's no need. The Grand Master is too lily-livered to take any action against me. But tell me, who really sent you here?'

'You can tell the Grand Master it was El Capitán de Diablo who has deprived him of his precious chalice,' I lied. Anything to help send Diablo to hell or prison or both.

'Of course, Diablo,' muttered Black. 'That moron. He'll be the death of us all . . . yes, we'll all end like Rafe Swann.'

There was a dry, sardonic laugh. I think my heart stopped for a beat or two, and the skin all over my body became cold and creeping. I put my hand on my dagger.

'Rafe Swann? What do you want to go talking about him for?' My voice was hoarse, gravelly in my throat.

Black stared at me for what seemed to be a very long time. 'So it's true, eh? It's not just a passing resemblance? Well, I never. You must be Lily.'

'I don't know what you mean!' I pulled the dagger from my belt, my heart all anger now.

'You look like the ghost of him, girl.'

'Shut your mouth!'

'So now you're doing the bidding of the man who killed your father? It's a strange thing.'

I hit him.

He was the first person I ever hit, and just about the last, but I hit him with a fury and he fell to the floor. He still wouldn't shut up.

'You're too young to have blood on your hands.'

'I already have bloody hands,' I growled like a real pirate, and grabbed the musket, primed it, and aimed it at his chest.

'Indeed, quite the pirate princess.' He smiled again.

I could trust myself no longer with the gun in my hands, spun around and shot the library shutters off their hinges. I threw the musket into the fireplace with a crash. Somewhere in the house there were cries and shouted alarms. Like a flash, I leaped over Black, still sprawled on the floor, and scooped up an armful of books scattered across the desk.

'When you're ready to hear what happened to Swann, come back without your men, and if I'm still alive, I'll tell you the terrible truth.' Black was shouting now.

'I don't give a damn about Rafe Swann!'

I leaped over the shattered remains of the window and ran out into the night. Jem and the boys were racing back up the path.

'We heard a shot,' Jem panted.

'That was me — let's hop it.'

I could see them glance at each other and back at me, admiringly.

'I didn't shoot him, you idiots, I just made it seem like we're a much more fearsome lot of ruffians than we really are.'

'Speak for yourself, Cyg,' spluttered Miller as we thundered down the cliff path to the beach. 'We was fearsome enough until you came along.'

'You're pussycats, the lot of you — you can't fool me,' I teased, and we were all laughing, with relief as much as anything else, as we piled into the boat and struck out from the shore.

Jem was beside me in the stern, the books stacked up between us.

'Where is it?' I whispered.

'Right under you, stowed safe. What was all that business about the Grand Master and the change of plan?'

'I don't know, Jem. I was just making it up.'

He laughed aloud.

'Who the hell's that?' The surprise in Miller's voice made us all turn to face the shore. A lonely figure jumped up and down, waving his arms.

'Damn,' Jem swore, 'what fool got left behind?' He made ready to turn the boat.

'All hands are aboard, Jem,' said Miller. 'Don't know who that is, but he's not one of us.'

I grabbed the telescope from my pocket and trained it on the shore. In the half-light it was hard to tell, but it looked for all the world like —

'Carlo!'

Amid shouted greetings, we rowed back towards the beach. Carlo ran into the shallows to meet us, waving wildly.

'My friends!'

'Keep your voice down,' I hissed.

But Carlo's shouting was silenced as his feet

floundered on the rocky seabed. He wavered, struggled for balance like a beetle on its back, and then fell, diving face forward into the shallow water.

'No doubt about it,' said Miller. 'It's Carlo de Santiago.'

Carlo was laughing as we hauled him, dripping, aboard. Francesco slung an arm around his shoulders.

'So, little fish — we throw you out, and you swim back to us?'

Carlo's eyes shone happily. 'Where are we going next?' he asked, smiling around at us all.

'Who said you were coming with us?' Jem's sombre voice cut through the laughter.

'But you must let me sail with you,' Carlo pleaded. 'I cannot stay a moment longer in my father's house.'

'This isn't a sailing school for young lords.'

'Let him stay,' said Francesco. 'He's a good boy, he works hard.'

'No,' said Jem, firmly. 'We want to stay in these waters a while longer. We can't do that with the whole Maltese fleet out searching for us.'

'Nobody will search for me,' Carlo retorted. 'You saw my father's face. He doesn't care if I live or die.'

'Not surprised,' muttered Miller. Francesco, irate, pounded Miller on the arm, Miller punched him back, and all at once the small boat erupted in shouts and shoving, rocking dangerously in the shallow waves.

'Stop it!' I yelled. Nobody took any notice. I had half a mind to tip them all overboard, as I'd done on my first night. I stood up and snatched the pistol from Jem's belt. The men fell silent.

'What are you doing, you fools?' I said. 'We're sitting here like fish in a rock pool. Get us back to the ship. Fast. We'll sort out Carlo later.'

Miller suddenly realised what I meant. All the windows in the house on the cliff were lit up now — soon the men of Black's household would charge down the hill, armed and angry.

'All right, you swabs,' he growled. 'Hands to oars.'

As they set to their oars, I sat down and handed Jem his pistol. Carlo was gazing at me with wide eyes. He wasn't smiling any more. I gestured to him to move closer.

'Carlo, who told you we would be here tonight?'

Jem looked astonished, the realisation only now taking hold.

'There was a note.'

'From who?'

'I don't know,' said Carlo. 'After, well . . . the morning after you came to visit my house, a note came. A message-boy brought it. The note wasn't signed. I thought perhaps it was from you.'

'The Turk?' Jem suggested.

I'd figured as much. But even Hussein Reis didn't know which night we'd choose for our raid. He must have spies all along the coast.

'We'd best keep Carlo with us for a while, Jem, and head back to Shipwreck Bay tonight.'

He nodded. 'And we'd better keep a sharper lookout from now on.'

13.
The deep blue sea

Jem's warning was quickly forgotten. By the time we'd sailed back around to Shipwreck Bay and dropped anchor the next day, we were all nearly asleep on our feet. I had a swim to try to wash the dust from my hair and clothes — the salt water stung the crystal cuts all over my face, hands and neck. When I dragged myself back on board, the crew of the *Mermaid* was fast asleep. Nobody was on lookout.

Those who'd been in the raiding party the night before were worn out, and the men who'd stayed on board had kept a restless watch. None of us had closed our eyes for two nights. Now the boys slept the sleep of the dead, sprawled across the deck or swinging below in their hammocks.

Down in the cabin, I carefully hung my sword on the hook set into the bulkhead and stared at it awhile, nudging it every so often to watch it spin, gracefully, in the air. Then finally I wrapped myself in a dry blanket and sat at the chart table, where Jem had stacked Mister Black's books. He'd also wedged the chalice, still tied in a cloth, at the very back of the chart cupboard. I gently prised it out of its hiding place and unwrapped it slowly. It was such a bright yellow gold I could hardly believe it was real. All around the rim and the stem were jewels, in tiny clusters like flowers around larger, massive gems of all colours and shapes.

It was a treasure such as I'd never seen. No wonder Black had been willing to defend it with his life. I placed it carefully on the table with both hands, as I'd seen the priest do at Mass, a lifetime ago in the little stone church on Santa Lucia.

Almost as precious to me were the books. I sniffed the fine leather bindings, the rich dusty smell of ink on paper that wafted from an open page. These books would make life on board much more interesting. Perhaps I could teach Jem to read. I flipped over a few pages, ran my finger over the lines of print — some charts, intricate maps of an unknown shore, strange etchings of odd-shaped plants and creatures, unfamiliar weapons and half-naked people, perhaps Africans. Hussein would know who they were. He seemed to know everything — more than he let on.

Then there were richly bound volumes, printed in small type, with names of vaguely familiar places and long-dead emperors. *The Decline and Fall of the Roman Empire*, by someone called Gibbon. Volume Two. Volume Four. Volumes Five and Six. Damn. I hadn't picked up the whole set. I smiled to myself. There'd be no going back for them now.

Mister Black. His words were thrumming in my ears like funeral bells: 'Now you do the bidding of the man who killed your father.'

'The man who killed . . . ' My head must have fallen down onto my arms as sleep took me into strange realms of storms and lonely rock islands and a man with a wild red beard and Mama crouching over a fire in a cave on a hilltop. When I opened my eyes, there was sun at the window and Hussein Reis stood in its light with the chalice in his hands.

'About time you stirred,' said Jem, standing close by. 'You must've been tired — you've slept through two meals.'

Somebody must have carried me to my hammock while I slept. I stretched and yawned and splashed my face, while Jem told Hussein about the raid. Then I raced out to retrieve my clean clothes from the deck, where they hung, rigid in the salt air, from the rigging. It didn't seem right to receive guests in the cabin in my underdrawers and shirt, so I pulled on my breeches and scrambled back down the ladder.

Hussein was turning the chalice over and over in his pale hands, gazing intently at it. The stream of sunlight pierced the depths of the red and blue jewels as they caught the glow. Slowly, he twisted the stem until it came away from the cup.

'Aha!' he breathed. He glanced up at us and grinned at our horrified faces. 'Don't you worry, I can put it back together again.'

From his belt, he drew his thin, curved dagger, and with its tip edged a tightly coiled paper out of the hollow chalice stem.

'I'll be dumblustered,' I murmured. 'What is it?'

Hussein unrolled the paper and held it up to the sunlight. 'It's a map.'

'A treasure map?' asked Jem.

'No, but it's worth a pretty penny in some quarters.'

Hussein stared fiercely, first at Jem and then at me. His blue eyes seemed to search my very soul, but for what? Trust?

At last his gaze wavered and he sighed. 'Let's be seated,' he said. 'There's a great deal to discuss, and we must soon be on our way.'

'Best get on with it then,' said Jem.

'It's a pity you people have never learned the Ottoman way of doing business. We sit comfortably, drink apple tea, enquire after the health of our entire known acquaintances, drink more tea, and then, after some hours, we talk.'

'Sounds bloody boring to me,' muttered Jem.

'You're not a Turk,' I said to Hussein. It was hard to keep the harshness from my voice.

'I am now.'

His glance fell on the book propped open on the table. 'Well, well, Lily, you have some reading to do.' He fingered the pages, looked up, and smiled. 'I fear Mister Black will grieve the loss of his volumes of Gibbon far more greatly than the theft of this chalice.'

He draped himself across the only chair, carefully arranging his robe around him. 'I'm going to sit, anyway. If you wish to be uncomfortable, so be it.'

I pulled myself up to perch on the chart table, my feet swinging off the floor.

'I'll stand,' said Jem.

'Mister McGuire, you are nothing if not consistent.'

'So,' I interrupted, 'what about the map?'

'Yes, the map.' Hussein drummed his fingertips together lightly. 'It's not, I regret, a treasure map. It's a plan of the secret tunnels under Valletta, known only to the Grand Master.'

'So we can raid the Great Palace?' asked Jem, hopefully.

'So we can defend the city from the French army. It is planning a great invasion, and I intend to stop it.'

'What?' Jem was just about ready to explode.

'Who are you?' I tried to fix Hussein with the same kind of forceful stare he'd used on me.

'I am as you see.' He spread his hands, palms upwards.

'You know what I mean,' I said.

'And I choose to ignore you.'

'Are you a spy?' There. It was out in the open, the thought that had been drumming inside my head for days.

He simply looked away. 'Now, my dear girl, you are becoming impertinent. I shall simply draw a veil over that accusation. Let us continue.'

With that, he tucked the map deep into the folds of his clothes. I saw now that his normally spotless robe was grimy from days ashore, with a thick hem of dust around the bottom. His face was tired, and it was a day or so since he had shaved.

'Very well,' I said. 'How did you get away from the Duke?'

'And where's our ransom?' Jem chipped in.

'The ransom? Not even I could persuade the good Duke to part with gold in exchange for a beloved son.'

'It don't matter,' retorted Jem, 'since we've kidnapped the boy all over again.'

'McGuire, I know only too well the boy ran away of his own free will, and would do so again, no matter how many coins changed hands. He is, I fear, not a wise investment.'

'Why were you in the Old City that night?'

'Lily, please, as much as I admire your curiosity, this could go on for hours if you two keep asking random questions. Allow me to explain on my own terms.'

'Stop beating around the four winds, then,' Jem growled.

'There is much I cannot tell you,' said Hussein. 'Forgive me. But, all right, let's start with the Duke. He's a great patriot, and so, no doubt, is his son.'

'He's full enough of it, aye,' Jem nodded.

'The boy should go home, ransom or no ransom. Malta will need all its sons in the coming weeks. But I digress. I was there, when you so rudely interrupted, arranging delivery of —'

'Carlo?'

'No, this map,' he patted the place where it lay hidden, 'and also certain other objects that your men kindly removed from the Santa Lucia tower for us.'

'Those bloody guns,' said Jem.

'Guns?' I shouted, jumping down from the table. 'Is that what was in those bundles? Is that what all that shooting and killing was for? Just a few guns?'

'Calm down, Lily, please.'

'That's the night I was kidnapped. I'd still be at home, if it wasn't for those stupid guns!'

'I know,' said Hussein. 'It was an unforeseeable consequence. But perhaps one day you'll feel it turned out for the best.'

'That's highly unlikely.' I crossed my arms defiantly.

'These are special guns, Lily, a new kind of musket with an almost infallible firing mechanism, and tremendous range. They will revolutionise the art of war. It seemed to me our Maltese friends might need them more than the good people of Santa Lucia, so I persuaded Diablo to capture them. How was I to know he'd capture you as well?'

'We tried to throw her back,' said Jem. 'Honest.'

'He nearly blew up the whole town,' I said.

'Diablo is not the most subtle of men,' said Hussein. 'I'm sorry. Believe me, I would never send anyone to attack Santa Lucia. I know it well, and I grieve for any lives that were lost.'

I shook my head. The more he explained, the less clear it became.

'What does Diablo care if the French invade Malta? You can't tell me he's patriotic.'

'I doubt that he remembers which country he was born in,' said Hussein. 'He pretends to be a Spaniard, but I imagine he was born in a poorhouse somewhere in London town.'

Jem snorted. 'I had him down as a Portsmouth harbour rat, myself.'

'Whoever he may have once been,' Hussein went on, 'Diablo now cares only about his income. If the French invade, it'll be very bad for Diablo and his kind. Frankly, their days are over already, but they don't realise it.'

He smiled, just a little. 'You are entering the profession at a difficult time, Lily. The great days of piracy are over. The corsairs have retired to their harems. The Knights of Malta have been crippled by the revolution in Paris — all their assets have been seized, some of their greatest men have gone to the guillotine. These are desperate times for Europe. In such times, brave men die and evil men prosper. But if Napoleon's army takes over the Mediterranean, piracy will be finished forever.'

'Never!' snorted Jem.

'It makes sense,' I said. 'With a grand army comes a great fleet.'

'Not to mention an extremely efficient secret police,' Hussein went on. 'French judges, tribunals, bureaucrats, executioners, perhaps even officers who can't be bribed. Not good for Diablo, not good for the Knights of Malta. You, Master McGuire, might need to take up a different trade.'

Jem rubbed his whiskers. 'Always wanted to run a tavern. I been saving some gold.'

'Ah yes,' Hussein chuckled, 'the pirate's dream. A tavern full of women and beer. Your chance may come sooner than you think.'

'Then the Knights are in on this too?' I asked him. 'That's why you were meeting the Duke de Santiago that night.'

'Perhaps. Perhaps not. It's not as simple as that. Certainly some of the Knights will oppose the French, as will the old noble Maltese families, like de Santiago. But many Knights are French themselves. Their feelings on the matter are, to say the least, mixed.'

'It'll never happen,' said Jem. 'What do the French want with this old lump of rock?'

'My dear man, it is happening. The fleet is gathering in Toulon as we speak. This lump of rock may be nothing more than a stepping stone, but such stones do get stepped on, even by great men.'

There was a moment of thoughtful silence.

'How long have we got?' Jem asked.

'Weeks. Days. They may have set sail already. It depends, as always, on the winds.'

'You mean there's something you don't know?' Jem teased. 'How about that?'

Hussein smiled with him. 'Sadly, there is much I don't know, and no time to learn it.'

'What's in the Golden Grotto?' I asked, remembering Diablo poring over the chart, muttering into his beard.

'Nothing besides seaweed, but you've heard the rumours. Treasure upon treasure for the taking. It's a myth, as you well know, but Diablo will not let it rest.'

'Where the hell's he gone, then?' said Jem.

Hussein shrugged again. 'Who knows? I have sent my crew to intercept him. They have orders to bring him back here under guard or kill him. I don't care which. He has betrayed me once too often. He sailed off with the English guns, and any day now we will need them. Napoleon is on his way.'

Diablo — at gunpoint or dead. That meant . . .

'So I'm free?' I could hardly believe I could say the words.

'You are free of Diablo, at least — all of you,' Hussein said quietly.

All I knew at that moment was the sound of the air, in and out of my lungs, and the feel of the ship moving gently beneath my feet. I walked to the window and gazed out across the clear blue waters to the sunlit beach, where a few of the boys were lying about on the hot pebbles, their feet splashing in the shallows.

Behind me, Hussein was issuing orders.

'McGuire, you may inform the crew they are released from their bond with Diablo, as he has forfeited his captaincy. You may keep the *Mermaid*, in equal shares, as payment for services. If you choose to keep sailing her, rather than sell her, I may engage you on some irregular tasks, since you have proven yourselves brave and trustworthy enough, if a little rash at times. I will pay you, of course.'

Free. Who cared about Napoleon and the armies of Europe, the Golden Grotto, or the mysterious Knights of Malta? I was free.

But now what?

'I'll go tell the boys,' Jem said, grinning, 'then we'd best get out of here.'

He sprinted out of the cabin and up onto the deck, shouting, 'All hands on deck! Get those lubbers back on board. Sound the bell! Ready to make sail.'

Hussein, however, had not moved. He waited a minute or two until the noise from above died down, and then spoke to me gently.

'In a few days I will be sailing to Santa Lucia.' He held up his hand before I could even get any words out. 'No, Lily, I cannot take you with me. I travel on an old fishing boat.'

'But I've sailed all over these seas with just my little brother, in a much smaller boat.'

'Have you indeed?' he asked, one eyebrow slightly raised. 'Nothing would surprise me. But you do me too much credit. I wasn't worried about your safety, but my own. Your presence would make me far too conspicuous.'

'Oh, I see.' I paced the cabin, from the narrow door to the window and back. Before me, to the north, spread the endless ocean.

'But if you need me to convey a message to anyone, I would be happy to do so.'

Happiness tore at my heart. Funny how it does that — how you can get so happy it actually hurts.

'Really? Anyone?'

'Anybody at all. It's the least I can do, in return for you bringing me this map — although I also have some more practical payment at hand.'

He untied an old brown purse from his belt and threw it on the table. It made a lovely clinking sound.

'It was gold that you requested, wasn't it? Not quite as much as Carlo's ransom, but enough to share around. Now write your note, and I'll be on deck when you're ready. But don't take too long.'

Pirate gold, and well-earned, too, even if I did say so myself. I pushed it aside for a moment and sat, alone now, in the dark cabin, scribbling as fast as I could. When I'd finished, I rolled up the paper and tied it with one of the bookmark ribbons from Mister Black's books. By the time I reached the deck, the crew had gathered and swung into action, and

Hussein was standing in the bows, watching the horizon.

'Here,' I said. 'You promise to deliver it?'

'I promise.' He took the letter from me and turned it over to read the name I had scrawled on the front.

'It's halfway up the hill, above Battery Point,' I said, 'just a tiny house, on the left.'

He smiled down at me. 'Don't worry, I'll find it.' He smoothed my letter between his fingers and tucked it inside his robe, beside the precious map of underground Valletta.

As we edged out of the bay to seek an offshore breeze, Hussein stayed in the bow, looking out to sea and sometimes glancing up into the sails approvingly. I was proud of this ship, proud of the boys who handled her so nimbly, of Jem and his mastery of the sails. I was pleased that the haughty Hussein was seeing the boys at their best, heaving together on the sheets, laughing and singing at their work — Max at the tiller straining to bring the *Mermaid* around, Jem with his eyes on the sails, the currents, and the invisible wind.

I climbed high up the mast after we hauled tight the mainsail — stayed aloft and gazed around, along the bay and deserted beaches, up along the dry headlands, and across the heaving ocean. I had to admit then, for the first time, that I was also proud of myself for being a part of this crew. I had a mighty sword, a purse of gold, and a place in a ship.

There was a cheer from the deck, so I glanced around, surprised. Brasher had finally finished his needlework: above me, from the top of the mast, streamed our new pennant, red with gold edging, and instead of a fearsome skeleton or grinning skull, there fluttered a beautiful golden mermaid.

I climbed down. There was work to do. My feet hit the deck with a thump. Max scowled. He'd told me off a thousand times for dropping the last yard down the rigging, but I always forgot, and the sound of my landing always woke whichever poor soul had just got to sleep in a hammock below deck. Today I just grinned.

'Cyg!' Jem called. 'Set the course. What say we drop Hussein around near Mġarr, and then make our way to Sicily?'

'Sicily?' Francesco and Ricardo were beside themselves with glee.

'Sounds good to me,' Miller nodded. He clambered up the ropes to go on watch. He had the best eyes of us all. Miller could tell you not only the shape of a distant sail, but the kind of ship she was, the port she sailed from, and probably the name of the captain's daughter.

Sicily was a long way from Santa Lucia. But I had made my choice.

So had Carlo. 'I too will leave the ship at Mġarr,' he said, quietly.

'But your father?'

'If the French are really coming, my father will need me.' He smiled, but sadly. 'Even if he does not feel it.'

Jem touched Carlo lightly on the shoulder. 'I reckon it's best. You'll have your work before you, fighting off old Napoleon.'

'Fighting off old nappy-on,' Brasher snorted. 'Whoever heard of such a thing?'

But as the boys around us sniggered, Miller's cry from the mast sounded out loud and clear.

'Sail ho!'

'Where away?' asked Jem.

'Sail ho!' Miller called again.

'We heard you,' shouted Brasher.

'Sail ho! And sail . . . oh my God!' Miller cried.

'What is it?' shouted Jem.

Miller simply pointed. We all wrestled for the telescope.

Jem peered through it for a moment, then handed it to me and ran to speak with Hussein. I put the glass to my eye. There, ranged all along the horizon, were sails, hundreds of them. An entire navy.

The French fleet.

'All hands!' Jem shouted from the bow. 'Make sail!'

He raced the length of the deck.

'Set a new course, Cyg. Hussein wants to be taken direct to the Knights in the White Tower, to give the alarm. Then we'd better get the blazes out of here.'

So the *Mermaid*, with her red and gold pennant flying, all canvas spread, and an Irish Turk standing in the bow, rounded the headland and fired all her cannon to warn the people of a tiny island that their destiny was on the horizon.

So was ours. But that's another story.

Dear Mama,

I am alive and unharmed (mostly), although I did accidentally get kidnapped by pirates. I hope you haven't been too worried. I miss you both so much it hurts me inside, and I've cried through the night, just like you, I'm sure.

I'm on a fine new ship now. I wish Lucas could see her, under full sail in a stiff breeze. I'm the navigator, one of the crew, so they don't treat me badly any more. I've met men who know of my father — which means he may be alive somewhere. I have sworn to find out the truth, then you won't despair any longer.

You were wrong about one thing, Mama. Pirates are not just pirates. Sometimes they are sailors who can't make a living any other way. They are not always evil, just poor and desperate. The men I sail with are like that, and I am safe enough now. They look after me and I look after them.

So you must not fret. I will stay a while longer on the Mermaid, to see if I can make our fortunes somehow. One fine day I will return to you, with some gold in my pocket, and you will marvel at my adventures. We will laugh, and you will stroke my hair, and I will never leave you again.

Who knows? I may even bring my father home with me.

I long for that day.

Your loving daughter,

Lil

Seafaring words of the Mediterranean

Abeam: Beside a ship, side on — for example, another ship drawing up next to you.

About ship: An order to change direction or come about. 'Ready about' means everyone needs to get ready to change the angle of the sails.

Admiral: The most senior commanding officer of the Navy, appointed by the Admiralty. The next in rank is a Vice-Admiral, followed by a Rear Admiral. Any sort of admiral may be in command of a fleet and hoist his pennant in a flagship.

Admiralty: The British government ministry in charge of the Royal Navy.

Aft: Towards the stern or back end of the ship

Aloft: Above. To 'go aloft', you climb up the ratlines to set sails, watch for other ships, or repair rigging.

Articles of War: Official rules governing conduct on all British Navy ships.

Astern: Behind the ship.

Avast: An order to stop doing what you're doing (rowing or hauling).

Aweigh: The anchor is clear of the water ('Anchors aweigh' means the anchor is weighed or clear and the ship can sail on).

Ballast: Rocks, iron or even cargo loaded onto a ship to keep it stable.

Barbary Coast: The North African states of Tunis, Tripoli and Algiers, which by 1798 were part of the Muslim Ottoman Empire. These cities supported fleets of corsairs to attack the ships of Christian countries such as France, Spain and England, just as the galleys of the Knights of Malta attacked those of the Barbary States.

Bastion: Part of a fort or castle that sticks out from the walls, allowing guns to be fired along the wall.

Batten down: Close all deck hatches and secure gear in bad weather.

Beam: Across the middle or the widest part of a ship.

Beating: Zigzagging so the ship can move forward against the wind.

Becalmed: Unable to move because there isn't any wind.

Belay: An order to stop hauling, or make fast. A belaying pin is a carved spike around which lines are tied or made fast.

Bilge: The hollow section inside the lower part of the ship or boat (and the smelly water that collects in it).

Biscuit: Same as **Hardtack**.

Blunderbuss: A gun with a short, wide barrel, almost trumpet-shaped, handy for boarding ships.

Bonġu: Good morning (in Maltese).

Bonswa: Good evening (in Maltese).

Booty: Loot, like cargo, weapons and any treasure or goods found on a ship. Ships taken by pirates were usually sold off, and the proceeds were included in the booty. Every pirate in the crew (or their family, if the pirate had died in the battle) was given a share.

Bosun: (short for 'boatswain') The senior crew member in charge of organising the crew on deck and their equipment.

Bow: The front or forward end of a ship.

Bowsprit: A pole pointing out almost horizontal from the bow to carry spritsails.

Braces: On a square-rigged ship like *Gisella*, the braces are cables pulled so that the square sails twist around on the mast.

Brigantine: A ship with at least two masts, square sails on the foremast, but fore-and-aft sails on the mainmast. It's a square-rigged ship, but has triangular sails as well, so it can sail in different directions. *Gisella* is a brigantine.

Broadside: All the cannon on one side of the ship firing at once.

Bulkheads: Walls inside a ship (not part of the hull), some of which can be removed easily to make room for battle or cargo.

Cannonade: A blast of continuous gunfire.

Capstan: A barrel-shaped winch with handles, to lift the heavy anchor.

Carronade: A powerful, squat-barrelled cannon.

Chart: A map of the coast and seas, including shoals, rocks and other dangers.

Clear for action: The order to get ready for battle. The crew clears the deck of any loose or spare equipment, runs out the cannon and lashes them, gets gunpowder and cannonballs ready, and makes sure the ship is in fighting order.

Close-hauled: Sailing as close as possible to the wind.

Come about: Turn the ship or boat into or across the wind.

Compass: An instrument with a magnetised needle or pointer that always points north.

Corsair: A pirate licensed to attack other ships,

like those of the Barbary States, or sailing from Malta under the protection of the Knights. English and American corsairs like Sir Francis Drake were usually called 'privateers' and they carried a 'letter of marque' to prove they were allowed to attack other ships.

Course: The sailing direction set by the navigator or captain. The course is named so the ship sails towards one of the points of the compass, for example, southwest.

Cutlass: A sturdy, heavy-bladed sword with a rounded knuckle-guard, used by sailors and pirates.

Dey: The Ottoman governor of Algiers. Each of the major Barbary States was independently ruled.

Dory: A light, narrow sailing and rowing boat. Lucas and Lily's dory, the *Swallow*, has two masts.

Downwind: Away from the wind.

El Capitán: Captain (in Spanish).

Fathom: A measurement of depth, equal to six feet (or roughly two metres).

Figurehead: A carved statue on the prow of a ship. The *Mermaid*, naturally, has a mermaid figurehead.

Flagship: The ship in a fleet which carries its commanding admiral. The flagship flies a pennant to show other ships that the admiral is on board.

Fleet: A group of more than ten warships.

Flotilla: A small group of warships.

Fore-and-aft rig: Triangular sails rigged along the ship (not across it, like a square-rig).

Foremast: The mast forward or in front of the mainmast.

Foresail: The largest sail on the foremast.

Forward: Towards the bow or front of the ship (opposite of aft). Pronounced 'forrard'.

Frigate: A warship with three masts and a bowsprit, a raised quarterdeck, and 24–38 guns along one gun deck.

Gaff-rig: A fore-and-aft sail mounted on a light pole at the top.

Galley: The elegant, oar-driven warships of the great naval fleets of Barbary, Venice and Malta, often powered by slaves. The galley is also the name of a ship's kitchen, usually not much more than a fireplace and a couple of cauldrons.

Gibbet: Gallows where the bodies of people executed for crimes of piracy were left chained and hanging above the water, as a warning to other pirates.

Guinea: A British coin, worth 21 shillings. (Guinea is also the name of the country in west Africa where the gold to make the coins was mined.)

Gun ports: Holes in the side of a ship through which the cannon fire. Gun ports have a flap over them to keep the water out when the guns aren't being used.

Gunwales: The rim around a ship or boat, like a handrail. Pronounced 'gunnells'.

Halyard: The rope used to raise or lower a sail.

Hands: Crew members, especially those who actually work the sails. 'All hands on deck' means that every available crew member is needed to help out.

Hardtack: Dry, solid ship's biscuit made of flour. On long voyages, especially on navy ships, hardtack was the only staple food, and became infested with weevils (grubs).

Hawser: A short rope or cable, often used for securing cannon.

Heave to: Stop a ship. Once she's stopped, she is 'hove to'.

Helm: The steering. 'Helm's a-lee' means you have brought the rudder right around, when you are changing tack or coming about.

Hold: The cargo or storage area below decks (on a big ship, the hold is several levels down).

Holystones: Sandstone blocks, about the size of a Bible, used to grind away dirt from the deck.

Hull: The planking that makes up the body of a ship.

Idlers: Crew members who are not part of the watch, such as carpenters and sail-makers.

***Isola*:** Island (in Italian).

***Iva*:** Yes (in Maltese).

Jib: Small triangular sail at the bow of a yacht or ship.

Knights of Malta: The Sovereign and Military Order of the Knights Hospitaller of St John of Jerusalem ruled Malta from 1530 to 1798.

Knots: Measurement of a ship's speed: 1 knot equals 1 nautical mile per hour.

Larboard: The left-hand side of a ship or boat, as you look forward (known later as 'port').

Lateen sail: Large, squarish sail hung from a pole from the mainmast. A lateen sail runs along the ship, from the mainmast to the stern.

League: A measurement of distance, equal to three nautical miles.

Lee: The side of a ship or boat away from the wind.

Letter of marque: Officially known as a 'letter of marque and reprisal', this was an official government letter authorising a captain to 'subdue, seize and take armed' any ships owned by countries who were enemies. It was government-approved piracy. See **Corsair**.

Line: The ropes used to haul sails into position.

Log: The book in which the captain or navigator writes the ship's position and progress. A log is also a lump of wood dropped over the side of the ship and then hauled back in after the ship has sailed past it, to measure a ship's speed by the number of knots in the rope.

Lubbers: People who live on land, or who are not used to sailing.

Mainmast: The central and tallest mast on any ship. If there is more than one mast, in front of the mainmast is the foremast, and behind it is the mizzenmast.

Make fast: Tie off or secure a rope.

Maltese: The language of Malta.

Mast: The tall poles that stick up from the deck of a ship and hold the sails. The poles horizontal across the mast are the yards. A sailing ship may have up to six masts — the *Mermaid* has one mast; *Gisella* has two.

Merħba: Hello (in Maltese).

Mizzenmast: The smaller mast at the rear of a ship.

Navigator: The navigator on a ship figures out and records the ship's position, estimates the speed of the ship and the distance to be covered, and sets the course. In 1798 navigators used a compass, charts of known coastlines and waters, a sextant or quadrant, and mathematics to help determine the ship's position.

Ottoman Empire: One of the largest and longest-lasting empires ever to rule around the coast of the Mediterranean Sea, it rose out of Turkey and existed from 1281 to 1923. At its greatest, it ruled an area of nearly 12 million square kilometres. From 1517, when it conquered Palestine and Egypt, and the Holy City of Mecca, it was an Islamic state.

The Sultan or ruler of the Empire was also the Caliph or official guardian of Islam. The later Crusades were fought by European states against the Ottoman Empire. See **Barbary Coast**.

Packet: A fast ship carrying mail and passengers on regular routes.

Portcullis: Heavy grating that slides up and down, as a gate on a castle or fort.

Press: Navies forced (or pressed) sailors into service, by tricking, bribing and even kidnapping men from other ships or from villages along the coast. The crew that rounded up the men was called a 'press gang'.

Prow: The pointed front of a ship, often decorated with a figurehead.

Quadrant: An instrument used by navigators for measuring the angle of the sun (or stars) above the horizon, to help determine a ship's position.

Quarterdeck: A raised platform or top deck at the stern of a larger ship. This is where the captain stands.

Ramparts: A fort or castle wall that is thick enough to have a walkway along the top.

Rapier: A fine-bladed thrusting sword, often highly decorated, used by nobility or officers.

Ratlines: Rope ladders made by tying short ropes across the shrouds, so you can climb up a mast.

Reef sails: To tie up a sail, so that it isn't showing as much canvas. You reef sails or reduce canvas in a big wind, to make sure you can still control the ship.

Reis: A captain in the Barbary and Ottoman fleets. 'Hussein Reis' means 'Captain Hussein'. Sometimes spelled *rais*, or in Turkish: *raïs*.

Rig: The design of the sail system (such as a square-rig or brigantine rig).

Rigging: The ropes and cables that make up the rig. The standing rigging (such as shrouds or stays) holds up the masts and is painted with tar to protect it. Running rigging (including halyards and sheets) is used to lower and raise the sails and yards, and it is not tarred.

Rowlocks: Semicircles of brass that hold the oars in place in a rowboat. Pronounced 'rollicks'.

Rudder: A long plank or fin, turned in the water by the tiller or wheel, which steers the ship.

Schooner: A fast, narrow ship with two masts. Usually gaff-rigged, with a large sail on the mainmast and a headsail and jib attached to the bowsprit.

Scimitar: A North African sword with a long curved blade. Hussein Reis and his men bear scimitars.

Scow: A flat-bottomed ship or boat used for carrying cargo, especially in coastal areas and on rivers.

Scuppers: Holes carved into the sides of boats or ships, above the deckline, to let water escape.

Scurvy: The disease that killed thousands of sailors on long voyages, because they didn't eat fresh fruit or vegetables. Scurvy is caused by a lack of vitamin C.

Sheets: Ropes attached to the bottom corners of sails, which you pull to adjust the sails' tightness and direction.

Ship of the line: A warship powerful enough to take its place in the line of battle. The Royal Navy classified its ships by rating them according to how many cannon they carried. There were six levels of rating, and any ship rated three or over (meaning it had more than 64 guns) was a ship of the line. The biggest and best were the first-rates. A ship of the line carried hundreds of crew and had two or three gun decks. Ships of the line often sailed in fleets with smaller, faster frigates, and in battle sailed in towards the enemy in a line, firing sideways.

Shrouds: Tarred ropes that support the mast.

Skiff: A light, narrow row boat.

Skużani: Excuse me (Maltese).

Sloop: A small, speedy ship with one mast, sometimes gaff-rigged, with a huge mainsail and an equally vast triangular foresail fixed to a long bowsprit. The *Mermaid* is a sloop, and so are many modern yachts.

Slow match: Slow-burning fuses used to set off gunpowder and fire cannon.

Spar: A long timber pole (such as a yard).

Spritsails: Sails at the very front of a ship — above the bowsprit.

Square-rig: A ship rigged with square or rectangular sails arranged across the width of the deck. Admiral Nelson's flagship, HMS *Victory*, was a first-rate square-rigged ship with 102 cannon on three gun-decks. See **Ship of the line**.

Starboard: The right-hand side of a ship or boat, as you look forward.

Stays: Part of the standing rigging, stays are ropes that run forward from a mast, to help support it.

Staysails: Triangular fore-and-aft sails attached to the stays.

Stern: The rear or back of a ship.

Swab: A mop or cloth used to wash the decks. 'Swabber' is slang word for sailor.

Tack: To change the ship's direction, by turning the bow through the wind.

Tar: A thick, black liquid painted onto standing rigging to protect it. It is also used to make pitch, painted on canvas for waterproofing. Sailors who had served in the navy were called 'tars' because they spent so much time tarring the ropes.

Taridha: Fast, narrow Arab ship, with one mast and a lateen sail. Up to sixteen oars on each side meant the ship didn't have to wait for the wind. Known to English sailors as a 'tartan'.

Thwart: A seat, made from planks set across the boat.

Tiller: The wooden lever or bar used to direct the steering gear. Larger ships are controlled by a wheel.

Tops: The platform at the masthead, used for a lookout. In warships, large platforms hold several sharpshooters each — these are called 'fighting tops'.

Topsail: A sail above the gaff, or on a topmast.

Trim the sails: Make sure the sails are placed to get the most speed out of any wind.

Watch: The crew were rostered on duty in groups, or watches — one watch worked while the other slept and ate. To be on watch is also to be on the lookout for danger or other ships.

Weigh anchor: Lift the anchor clear of the water.

Winds: A wind is named according to the point of the compass from which it blows. For example, a wind blowing from the north is a north wind. Some seasonal winds in the Mediterranean Sea have traditional names based on the compass points, like the springtime southeasterly which blows across from North Africa, called the *xlokk* in Malta, but more famous in Italian as the *sirocco*.

Windward: The direction the wind is coming from ('leeward' is the direction the wind is going). Also means the side of the ship facing the wind.

Yard: A timber pole or spar set across a mast to carry a sail.

Yardarm: The ends of a yard.